THE FLYING SAUCER STORY

Brinsley Le Poer Trench

SAUCERIAN PUBLISHER
Original Sources in Ufology

ISBN: **978-0-9827964-2-9**

2022, Saucerian Publisher

PROLOGUE

It is generally a good idea to return to the classics in any genre. This also goes for UFO literature. Rereading a book, or reviewing old documents after ten or twenty years is a rewarding experience. You will discover new data and ideas you didn't notice before. The reason, of course, is that you are, in many ways, not the same person reading the book the second or third time. Hopefully you have advanced in knowledge, experience, intellectual and spiritual discernment. A good starting point is to reread the contactee classics material in order to understand the deeper mystery involved in what happened during that era.

William Francis Brinsley Le Poer Trench (September 18, 1911 - May 18, 1995) was a British saucerian, notably active as an editor of the *Flying Saucer Review* and involved in several ufo groups, including the *International Unidentified Object Observer Corps, Contact International, and the British UFO Research Association (BUFORA)*, among others. Further to his personal work, Le Poer Trench used his peerage as the Earl of Clancarty and accompanying seat in the United Kingdom's House of Lords to press his government for releasing information regarding UFOs and organized the "The House of Lords UFO Debate" of January 1979.

This is the *Flying Saucer Story.* The most exciting and the most wonderful saga of all time. It brings you the truth so long withheld from us that millions of planets in this universe is inhabited and that space ships from other worlds have been visiting our planet Earth for centuries, possibly millennia. Evidence has shown that for thousands upon thousands of years, other civilizations in this galaxy have been masters the technical problems of interstellar fly. The book's contents are well documented and discuss the reports of more than 2,000 landings since 1947.

This book is a facsimile reproduction of the original printed text in shades of gray of 1966. Because this material is culturally important, we have made it available as part of our commitment to protect, preserve and promote knowledge in the world. This book has been formatted from their original version for publication. **IMPORTANT, although we have attempted to maintain the integrity of the issues accurately, the present reproduction could have missing and blurred pages poor pictures due to the age of the original scanned copy.** Because this material is culturally important, we have made it available as part of our commitment to protect, preserve and promote knowledge in the world.

Editor
Saucerian Publisher

You are all familiar with an ordinary telephone directory. You want to speak to someone, you look up his number, and you dial the appropriate code. My speculation is that a similiar situation exists, and has existed for billions of years in the Galaxy. My speculation is that an interchange of messages is going on, on a vast scale, all the time, and that we are as unaware of it as a pygmy in the African forests is unaware of the radio messages that flash at the speed of light around the Earth. My guess is that there might be a million or more subscribers to the galactic directory. Our problem is to get our name into that directory.

PROFESSOR FRED HOYLE

Plumian Professor of Astronomy
Cambridge University

(Extract from his book OF MEN AND GALAXIES)

THE FLYING SAUCER STORY

Brinsley Le Poer Trench

CONTENTS

ACKNOWLEDGMENTS

I wish to thank Mr. Charles Bowen, the editor o
Flying Saucer Review, for permission to quote exten
sively and for his much appreciated co-operation.

Heinemann Educational Books Ltd., London, for thei
courtesy in allowing me to quote from Professor Fre
Hoyle's book *Of Men and Galaxies.*

Finally, I wish to warmly thank K. Dorn, of Shirley
Long Island, NY, USA, for considerable research note:
and for much assistance in correcting the manuscript.

PART ONE

THE EVIDENCE

Ah! if our sight was piercing enough to discover, where we only see brilliant points on the black background of the sky, resplendent suns which revolve in the expanse, and the inhabited worlds which follow them in their path, if it were given to us to embrace in a general coup d'oeil these myriads of fire-based systems; and if, advancing with the velocity of light, we could traverse from century to century, this unlimited number of suns and spheres, without ever meeting any limit to this prodigious immensity where God brings forth worlds and beings; looking behind, but no longer knowing in what part of the infinite to find this grain of dust called the Earth, we should stop fascinated and confounded by such a spectacle, and uniting our voice to the concert of universal nature, we should say from the depths of our soul: Almighty God! how senseless we were to believe that there was nothing beyond the Earth, and that our abode alone possessed the privilege of reflecting Thy greatness and power!

CAMILLE FLAMMARION

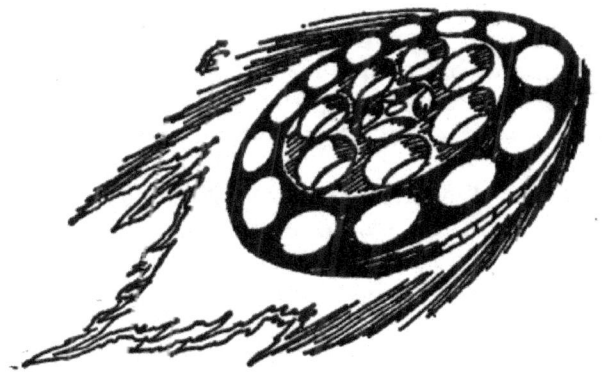

I

THIS IS THE Flying Saucer Story. The most exciting and wonderful saga of all time. It brings to you the truth so long withheld from us that millions of planets in this universe are inhabited and that space ships from other worlds have been visiting our planet Earth for centuries, possibly millennia.

When soon after World War II reports of flying saucers started appearing in the press, it seems most people dismissed them as arrant nonsense. Perhaps it was that mankind had been told for so long he was the supreme creation in the universe that the shock of having to share the priority with others was more than he could accept overnight. On the other hand, the reaction may have reflected nothing more than fear of the unknown. We don't know. We only feel on the whole propaganda on the subject has been handled very badly, driving countless individuals away who might otherwise have been genuinely interested. And we believe these may well comprise a large segment of the public who do not share the so-called "normal" fear of the unknown.

Invariably, these are the people who have always

been irresistibly drawn to the wonders of the night sky twinkling with myriad stars, and who have pondered over the possibility that some of them might be suns much like our own going about the inexhaustible business of furnishing life to billons of people just like ourselves.

These are the ones to whom it would seem utterly incredible if in this whole universe the only planet capable of supporting our form of life was this little world we call Earth. To them such a thing would make a mockery of Creation.

Could anyone possibly envision a useless wasted world, a world unenhanced by living creatures, or unenhanced by life of some form, organic or otherwise?

We wouldn't suggest for a moment that all planets are inhabited or even habitable. A planet, after all, is a living thing. It is born; it has a life span—although considerably longer than yours or mine. During its young days, of course, it is not possible for our form of life to exist upon it, and the same is true of its old age. However, a very large percentage of planets are middle-aged and, therefore, quite likely to be inhabited, especially when the mean distance from their sun is approximately the same as ours. The necessary distance, of course, will depend largely on the size and mass of their particular sun.

More and more scientists are now advancing the view that there is intelligent life in the universe. Recently, Dr. Harlow Shapley, the doyen of American astronomers; Sir Bernard Lovell, Director of the Jodrell Bank Radio Telescope, and Professor Fred Hoyle, Plumian Professor of Astrology at Cambridge University, have all given their considered opinion that millions of planets in our own galaxy—the Milky Way—may be inhabited.

Our own galaxy contains 100,000 million stars and our modern radio telescopes have observed more than 100,-000 million other galaxies stretching away in all directions. We know very little yet about the universe, but one thing is clear: the Creator obviously didn't have a chicken coop in mind when He created it!

July 23, 1965, marked the 100th anniversary program of *Sky at Night*[10] a regular program on BBC TV Channel I, in which Patrick Moore, the well-known astronomer, author and television star, talks about the night sky. To mark the occasion that evening the theme was 'communication with other worlds.' Others who took part were Desmond King-Hele, of the Royal Air Force Establishment, Farnborough, Dr. Frank Drake, of the Green Bank Radio Observatory, West Virginia, and Professor J. Shlovsky, of the Sternberg Institute, Moscow.

Desmond King-Hele suggested that out of the 100,-000 million planets in our Milky Way galaxy there could be 10,000 million stars with planets. He considered half of these might be habitable and half again supporting other forms of life. This still leaves 500 million planets with life in our own galaxy!

Now we have acquired all our much vaunted technology within the past two hundred years. For centuries prior to that we had been content to rely to a very great extent on the horse and the wheel.

If we assume that the Earth is only an average planet in development (and that may well be giving us ideas above our station!) then there must be millions of planets in the galaxy with far, far more advanced technologies than our own. When you think of the wonders we have achieved in just 200 years, imagine what other planets may have achieved in a thousand or ten thousand years, or even longer! It's an awesome thought.

So, the idea that people could come here from other planets outside our solar system is not particularly as-

---

*The numerals in the text refer to the Bibliography at the end of the book.

tonishing. When you think about this, it would seem much more incredible if they could not do so.

Most people have difficulty appreciating any position or standpoint other than what is offered by the current scientific know-how enjoying the popularity of the times. Few are gifted with vision. What we know today, and what we shall know tomorrow is almost certain to be quite different. What we know now in the various fields of technology compared to what we knew 300 years ago is truly fantastic.

Although there's no doubt within a relatively short time we'll be landing space ships on the Moon and Mars (Venus and the more remote planets of this system a little later), nearly everyone believes this will be the extent of our exploration of space, for it will be impossible for us to reach other solar systems because of the vast distances involved.

It is the same old story. Once, expert opinion held that athletes would never be able to run the mile in under four minutes—the human constitution couldn't stand it. Yet it did! Several Olympics' champions have come huffing and puffing down the track breaking the four-minute barrier on many occasions.

Not too many years ago, also, the world and its 'experts' were positive there'd never be any such thing as a 'flying machine.' Why, just anybody knew such a 'contraption' weighed down by a heavy engine couldn't get off the ground. They were proved wrong. The Wright brothers, and others engaged in similar pursuits, may not have startled the birds with their competition, but clear the ground they did!

Nothing is impossible. As Admiral Halsey said: "The impossible only takes a little longer."

When we come to have control over gravity and inertia, and over problems created by a vacuum and by MHD (magnetohydrodynamics) and have produced 'photon engines' (even now in experimental stages), we shall be able to travel faster in space than we ever dreamed—indeed, fast enough to reach the stars.

Evidence has shown that for thousands upon thousands of years other civilizations in this galaxy have been masters of all these technical problems and many more. For us, space travel is just beginning. We have much to learn, and if all continues well as it has during the past years we, too, shall return their visits.

Many people say, "Well, if these saucers are real, why haven't they landed? Why haven't we heard from these space people?"

A good question, and there's an equally good answer

They have visited us and they have landed. In fact, there are reports of more than 2,000 landings since 1947. These are discussed later in this book.

The reasons why they have not landed openly, we believe, are due mainly to the fact that their intentions most surely would be misunderstood, even more than they are already. Secondly, it is due to our tardy sociological and technological development. For several thousand years, just in the field of technology alone, we had nothing at all to speak of, and compared to them were a very unenlightened and primitive peoples preoccupied with plundering and ravaging our planet as well as ourselves. We still do to a great extent, although it has taken a slightly different form. None the less, this has not been conducive to open contact, nor is it particularly so today. Yet, however badly we may be managing our affairs, we are still trying valiantly to stand on our own feet.

Quite naturally civilizations highly advanced technically, socially and culturally—and there are probably millions of them in this galaxy—will tend to seek out similar climates which provide common interests and friendly exchange. Dr. Jan Gardomski, Director of the Polish Observatory in Warsaw, has discovered sixteen comparatively nearby solar systems probably supporting life like our own. Four of them present far more perfect conditions for life than does our Earth and can be rated Grade A. On the basis of this one US Air Force spokesman considered us to be fifth rate by comparison, or Grade E. Therefore, if his assumption is correct, and it probably is, we have no recourse but to whittle and remodel ourselves into topnotch shape. It seems, we have always had our work cut out for us.

However, curiously enough there is some evidence to suggest that eons ago certain enlightened areas of this planet were in open contact with other worlds.[2] Then, from natural causes a physical catastrophe (perhaps more than one) engulfed the world, causing what few survivors there were to start over again in rather strained circumstances to say the least.

There are records dotting our history which tend to indicate space ships from other worlds have visited us from time to time. After the catastrophes, it could even be that in some instances we may have been re-seeded by a few of these people from other solar systems, which would result, we'd think, in their taking a personal interest in us. In any event, for a very long time, as you shall see, space ships have kept an eye on us, and perhaps for no other reason than the unalterable fact that *we are here* and, therefore, *belong to the whole.*

Then, in 1945 we exploded the atom bomb. Once we had unlocked the secrets of nuclear fission they knew we were on our way. Space travel would soon follow. Since that time the Earth has elicited much interest and has been under constant surveillance by our space neighbors.

II

THE United States Air Force began to take serious interest in saucers around 1947, although there is evidence that reports had been filed with them by responsible military pilots prior to that year.

They introduced the term 'Unidentified Flying Object'—UFO for short—to cover any object in the sky that was unknown. The two names, 'UFO' and 'Flying Saucer' have since become almost interchangeable, although the term 'flying saucer' is a bit of a misnomer because many of the objects have not been reported as saucer-shaped. Instead, their shapes have been described as cigar, star, crescent, doughnut, tadpole, triangle, rectangle, trumpet, oval, bubble, circular, and heel (like the flat heel of a man's shoe).

At least two of these shapes belong among our own experimental aircraft, and we suspect some of the others have been 'planted' (as in a series of drawings, for example) in an effort to elicit comment and thus weed out true sightings from those that are false or mistaken.

Be that as it may, there are several different kinds of propulsion systems in use among UFOs, which may tend to indicate:

(1) They come from different worlds.

(2) Like us, they use different models for different purposes.

(3) By joint agreement they have jerry-built a number of inferior craft (inferior, that is, for intersolar or intergalactic flight) which are more akin to our understanding and technical development and, therefore, serve as an indirect means of communication showing us what can be done, on the one hand, while making us feel a little knowledgeable, on the other.

It could be any one of these three, or all of them combined. However, you may be able to think of many more reasons. Be our guests!

As to official recognition of UFOs, on September 23, 1947, the Chief of the Air Technical Intelligence Center (ATIC) sent a letter to the Air Force Commanding General stating that ATIC had come to the conclusion that UFOs were 'real.'

In January 1948, the US Air Force established the first of many official projects to investigate UFOs. This was Project Sign at Wright-Patterson Air Force Base.

Then, in September 1948, ATIC sent a highly secret report to the Air Force Chief of Staff, General Hoyt S. Vandenberg, (which leaked out, of course) presenting their conclusions that UFOs were interplanetary! However, ATIC was asked to provide further evidence.[3]

In February of 1949 Project Sign was dissolved and a new one, Project Grudge, was established. The new code word reflected a mirrored image of the new policy adopted. UFOs continued to be investigated, but it had now become official 'policy' to promulgate the idea that saucers were *not* 'real.' (Right here we must tell you that the word 'real' in connection with UFOs has been overworked to such a degree it has long since worn through the treads and is currently sparking along on its rims!)

Early in 1951, Captain Edward J. Ruppelt was ensconced as head of a new project which eventually in March of the following year became known as Project Blue Book. Ruppelt remained in charge until September 1953.

The US Air Force continued to blow 'hot' and 'cold,' issuing one conflicting report after the other. No group, it seems, had ever worked harder to make it appear there were two separate factions at the Pentagon in total disagreement over matters of policy concerning this vitally important subject.

Amusingly enough, during this time the flying saucers paid an unexpected visit to Washington, DC, treating that capital to the rarest, most entertaining and exhilarating air show ever seen. In all seriousness USAF jets were scrambled, of course, to investigate them and give chase, which really means the saucers invited them to join the fun and games, because although the saucers out-maneuvered them at every turn without half trying, the jets managed to 'close in' on them several times—in other words, the saucers allowed them to do so. Nothing could have been more obvious. The whole saucer air show smacked of the way our grown-ups pretend to play games of 'tag' with small children. We needn't point out that if conquest had been the saucers' aim, then the jets, the capital city of America and the Eastern seaboard, at the very least, would have been destroyed instantly. Obviously, nothing could have been further from the minds of our space visitors.

In all, the air show comprised two days separated a week apart which resulted in nothing more than forcing the 'mercury' up a mere tenth of a degree. Officialdom had to say something and Major General J. A. Samford, then Director of US Air Force Intelligence, was ordered by General Nathan F. Twining (later Air Force Chief of Staff) to hold a press conference.

It was at that famous meeting that General Samford stated: "However, there have remained a percentage of the total in the order of twenty per cent of the reports that have come from credible observers of relatively incredible things."

Almost two years later, General Twining himself issued a statement that must have been composed by a committee, probably the same one that 'put together the camel'—because he said that the best brains in the United States (not common horse sense) were working on the UFO problem and that the Air Force found themselves unable to explain ten per cent of the sightings investigated. All of which caused an American to quip, "It is regrettable that horse sense has been at a premium in the States ever since the Army disbanded the cavalry!"

Then, as an encore, a very clever documentary film called appropriately *UFO⁴* was presented to the public. The reactions to this were even more entertaining in some ways than the real saucer air show.

From the standpoint of the dual policy the film was a huge success, but in 'Hollywoodese' it would have been tagged a colossal flop. Seating capacity and SRO (standing room only) never became a problem. Documentaries are not too popular anyway—at least they are not box office—and the Air Force had seen to it that the actual film of this real saucer in motion would require far more imagination on the part of the audience than visual apparatus. It was undoubtedly the worst they could dredge up out of their files. Needless to say, this short strip was the only one shown of a saucer in flight (or in any other way, for that matter). The rest of the movie devoted itself to showing blips of Washington's saucer air show on a radar screen and listening to the running commentary.

In England the policy of the Air Ministry has to some extent been on a par with that of the United States. However, it has not issued the 'hot' and 'cold' statements that have come out of the other side of the Atlantic. In fact, despite all evidence, the Air Ministry steadfastly maintains that all UFOs can be explained by people seeing birds, balloons, conventional aircraft, the planet Venus and Earth-made satellites. One thing is clear about the UK, in matters pertaining to UFOs, it can be said that its policy is both 'u'nited and 'k'onsistent.

The embarrassing part is that incidents such as the following continue to occur: Flight Lt. J. R. Salandin, flying a Meteor Mk 8 jet fighter over Southend at 16,000 feet on October 14, 1954, saw two circular objects streaking between two other Meteor planes high above him. When he turned to look through his windscreen Salandin was startled to see another similar object hurtling towards him at his own altitude. He said: "It was silvery in color, had a bun-shaped top, a flange like two saucers in the middle and a bun underneath, and could not have been far off because it overlapped my windscreen!" (A Meteor fighter's 37-ft. span just fills the windscreen at 150 yards.) Salandin also said that as the saucer closed in it changed direction and passed on the port side at tremendous speed.[5]

We'd dearly love to hear the British Air Ministry's explanation of that one! However, all government agencies realize the people of the world are likely to know far more about flying saucers than they, therefore, any speculation on their part would be foolish and even more embarrassing.

Since 1947 hundreds of thousands of people all over the world have seen the saucers. They have been witnessed by air force, commercial and civilian pilots: coastguards; police; naval and military personnel; farmers; missionaries; lawyers; doctors; businessmen; astronomers; actors, and even an ambassador. Impressive as the list is, actually the preponderance of reports has come from what the world loves to call 'the common man.' This, together with other behavior patterns which have been painstakingly collected tells us a great deal about the feelings and philosophy of the minds behind the flying saucers.

It seems evident that to them a mouse holds equal rank with a king, or put another way, since both are acceptable life-forms, neither has any rank whatsoever. Although this is quite different from the systems we live under and practice, even we have always maintained that any life-form functioning in its proper environment at its own gait and natural capacity is a 'thing of beauty' and a marvel to behold. In this respect a dichotomy has arisen between our thinking and practice.

It would seem that in Earth's valiant effort to organize man, systems and 'isms' evolved which have gradually become more highly involved than evolved, and like the rolling snowball threaten to become a devastating avalanche destroying everything in its path. This state of affairs can hardly be said to have done anything for man's beauty! So, until we find means to divert the avalanche, we unfortunately find ourselves in a better position to vouch for the mouse than the king.

Naturally enough, men and governments feeling so helplessly trapped sought refuge in what appeared to be the only available solutions: either escape (deaden) the blunder (sensation), or increase it beyond the point of being able to feel anything at all. Being a society disproportionately geared and organized for 'extroverts,' the latter means was inevitably chosen.

However, aside from the matter of flying saucers being turned into one of international policy on a very high level, propaganda attempted to make them into 'scapegoats' or 'fall guys.' Everything the imagination of man could think of has been adroitly pinned on them at one time or another—if possible—including the suggestion that they've been malevolently manipulating and controlling our minds by means of what is called 'mental telepathy.' Nothing could be more absurd. Actually, it is highly probable that they may well have telepathic abilities. We have, too, but have allowed them through our reliance on other means of communication to become dormant; although a few country folk still use them. Actually, aside from showing us what their electromagnetic propulsion systems can do, from neon (Aurora Borealis) effects to other ones upon electrical equipment of our own, such as car ignition systems, compasses, radio, television reception and the like (which have unnecessarily frightened some people who know nothing at all about flying saucers), they have been observed doing nothing more than what our own scientists are wont to do, gather soil samples, as well as some of both our fresh and sea water. All of this indicates intensive study of the basic chemistry responsible for our kind of life, including the electrochemical reasons behind our tardy development and seeming genius for getting into one miserable scrape after the other.

Obviously, this problem is neither man's fault nor theirs but purely an unfortunate, although natural outcome of our peculiar electromagnetic make-up which, of course, is not hopeless at all and can very well be set to rights at source level.

The problem at the moment is to bring the true situation to everyone's attention in order that in time we may put our 'galactic' heads together and by concerted effort remodel planet Earth into a Grade A world we can all safely enjoy to the full.

III

Now, I am going to outline some of the major sightings since 1947. I will include one for each year (with the exception of 1952—a vintage year—and so I have provided two for it). However, I have referred briefly to other important sightings in postscripts to a particular year. I have tried to spread the load over different parts of the world. There are still some people who think the saucers are some kind of American joke. This is not true as you will see from these pages. The fact is that the saucers have been seen over every country and over every ocean, as well as over the polar regions.

THE FLYING SAUCER STORY

1947

THE ARNOLD SIGHTING

Tuesday, June 24, 1947, was to be a most unusual day for Kenneth Arnold. He took off from Chehalis, Washington, in an airplane specially designed for mountain work. He was on a mercy mission to look for a lost C-46 Marine transport plane that had crashed somewhere in the Cascade Mountains.[6]

It was a lovely sunny afternoon and visibility was very good. Arnold was making a wide turn over the area when a very bright flash lit up the sides of the plane. He searched the skies all around his aircraft trying to spot from where the flash had originated. Suddenly, the flash occurred again and this time Arnold saw a formation of nine gleaming objects coming from the direction of Mount Baker. They were flying close to the peaks at what seemed a very fast speed.

Arnold studied the formation as they flew on towards Mount Rainier. He happened to be in an excellent position to triangulate their speed between the peaks of Mount Rainier and Mount Adams, and was astonished to discover that they were doing better than 1,200 m.p.h. —an incredible speed in 1947!

He noticed that although they flew in echelon formation, that is, in two parallel lines of five and four objects respectively, their flight was erratic. He described their motion later to reporters as being like "saucers skimming over water." The press headlined them as 'flying saucers' and the name has stuck ever since.

Arnold got the impression that the vivid blue-white flashes coming from the objects were caused by the reflection of strong sunshine on their metallic looking surfaces.

Postscript to Arnold's sighting . . .

On July 4, a few days after Arnold's sighting, Captain E. J. Smith, a veteran pilot of United Airlines took off in a DC-3 from Boise, Idaho. A few minutes after take-off both Captain Smith and his co-pilot, Ralph Stevens, spotted a formation of five saucers. They called the stewardess forward to watch the strange formation with them.

Suddenly, the five objects took off at tremendous speed and four more came in to view. We can't help wondering if these were the same ones Arnold had seen a few days earlier.

1948

CHILES AND WHITTED

This sighting is of particular interest in that Clarence S. Chiles and John B. Witted, pilots of an Eastern Airlines DC-3 were enabled to get a really close look at a UFO as it flashed past them.

They took off from Houston, Texas, on July 23, 1948, at 8:30 P.M. on the Houston, Atlanta to Boston run. At 2:45 P.M. twenty miles west of Montgomery, Alabama, they spotted what they mistook for a jet fighter streaking towards them.

"It was heading southwest," Chiles said, "exactly opposite our course. Whatever it was flashed down towards us with terrific speed. We veered to the left. It veered sharply, too, and passed us about 700 feet to the right. I saw then it had no wings."

Since the craft passed by on Whitted's side he got a good look at it. "It was about 100 feet long," he said, "cigar-shaped and wingless, about twice the diameter of a B-29 with no protruding fins."

Both he and Chiles agreed the cabin had the brilliance of a magnesium flare. They saw no occupants.

Chiles stated: "An intense dark blue glow came from the side of the ship and ran the entire length of the fuselage—like a blue fluorescent light. The exhaust was a red-orange flame, with a lighter color predominant around the edges."

Both agreed the flame extended behind the ship thirty to fifty feet. Chiles noticed that the snout looked like it had a radar pole extending out from it; and both noticed two rows of windows.

Chiles said: "As it went by the pilot pulled up as if he'd just seen the DC-3 and wanted to avoid us. At that point there was a tremendous burst of flame from the rear. It zoomed into the clouds, its jet wash rocking our DC-3." He estimated that its speed was somewhere between five and seven hundred miles an hour.

As the ship vanished Chiles went back to check the passengers. All were asleep except Clarence McKelvie who said he had seen a brilliant streak of light flash past his window, but it had gone too swiftly for him to catch any details. (Clarence McKelvie, at that time was assistant managing editor of the American Education Press.)

Postscript to Chiles and Whitted . . .

Four days prior to Chiles and Whitted's sighting a wingless cigar with two rows of portholes had been seen near The Hague, Holland, on July 20 on four different occasions by a large number of eye-witnesses.[7]

1949

THE TOMBAUGH SIGHTING

The distinguished astronomer, Professor Clyde W. Tombaugh, discoverer of the planet Pluto, was the witness of a UFO.[3]

It was at about 10:45 P.M on August 20, 1949, that Professor Tombaugh was enjoying the evening air outside his house at Las Cruces, New Mexico, with his wife and mother-in-law.

He happened to glance up directly overhead and was amazed to see six or eight greenish lights flying southwards at uniform speeds, which immediately suggested to him they might have been windows of some large flying object dimly outlined against the night sky.

Professor Tombaugh commented afterwards that in all his thousands of hours of night sky-watching he had never seen anything so strange. The UFO made no sound.

Postscript to the Tombaugh sighting ...

Many people have asked why it is that professional astronomers do not see flying saucers more often. The answer is that their telescopes are frequently focused for long periods on some distant star or nebulae millions of miles out in space and it would be impossible for them to sight a saucer.

However, many amateur astronomers who have small telescopes have seen UFOs in the Earth's atmosphere and many strange objects have been sighted in the vicinity of the moon. Additionally, many well-known astronomers have sighted saucers· unaided by telescopes. The late Dr. H. Percy Wilkins, noted lunar expert, had a sighting from an aircraft. During an airline flight on June 11, 1954, from Charleston, W.VA., to Atlanta, Georgia, when he caught sight of two bright oval-shaped objects hanging above a bank of cumulus cloud, he described them as looking like polished metal plates reflecting the sunlight. Suddenly, a third UFO appeared. While the two he had noticed first continued to sway gently above the clouds, the third began to move with increasing speed, described a curve and then disappeared behind another cloud.[8]

THE FLYING SAUCER STORY

On May 20, 1950, at the Lowell Observatory at Flagstaff, Arizona, Dr. Seymour L. Hess, well-known astronomer, happened to be studying weather conditions with the naked eye. Suddenly he observed a bright object in the sky and picked up his binoculars to scan it more closely. It turned out to be a disc speeding along through wisps of cloud against the wind. (Not that there's anything extraordinary about a craft traveling against the wind. It merely ruled out the possibility of the oval-shaped object being a balloon—Author.)[3]

1950

A FANTASTIC AIR CIRCUS

March 18, 1950, was a day that the citizens of the small town of Farmington, New Mexico, will never forget. Every important American newspaper told the story of how the sky over Farmington was literally filled with flying saucers.

With few exceptions the entire township of some 5,000 inhabitants, including the mayor, newspaper men and members of the highway patrol, breathlessly watched an air show to end them all. A fantastic air circus!

Countless saucers performed aerial acrobatics at speeds over 1,000 mph, showing incredible maneuverability and acute control in split-second timing by their ability to avoid collisions.[9]

Postscript to Farmington . . .

Between August 25-30, the following year, large numbers of UFOs were seen together again. This time successive formations of about thirty space craft sped silently across the sky each night. They were photographed by Carl Hart, Jr., and witnessed by hundreds of people, including four college professors.[7]

1951

MEXICO CITY

One morning during the summer of 1951 news reporters and photographers moved into the airport at Mexico City to meet a VIP from the United States. The group were all gathered waiting for the visitor when someone looked up and gave a shout. Three saucers were hovering over the airport at a height of about 5,000 feet.[10]

Immediately, the cameras went into action and many photographs, in color, black and white, stills and movies were taken. People poured out of the waiting rooms and restaurant, and several hundred had a fine view of the saucers before they darted off at high speed in a southerly direction. The story broke in the Mexico City newspapers the following day but there were no pictures. It was reported that these had been confiscated by both American and Mexican authorities who promised to release them for publication after a thorough study. To this day, however, they have never been published.

Postscript to Mexico City . . .

During the morning of July 14, 1951, at White Sands Missile Base, New Mexico, two radar operators picked up a fast moving UFO on their radarscope. At the same time a tracker watching a B-29 with binoculars saw a large UFO near the bomber. Still another observer who happened to have a 35-mm camera handy managed to shoot 200 feet of film of it. It was said the film showed a round bright spot, but just as in the Mexico City story the film disappeared and has never been seen since.[3]

28

1952

SAUCER OVER TOKYO

A little before midnight on August 5, 1952, began one of the most fascinating sightings to come out of the Far East.[7] The scene was Haneda Air Force Base, now Tokyo International Airport in Japan.

Two control tower operators going on night duty were walking across the runway towards the tower. Suddenly, they noticed a very bright light over Tokyo Bay. It was an exceptionally strong one. When they realized it was moving they raced to the top of the tower to get a good look at it through binoculars, while the other two still on duty joined in.

What they saw appeared to be a circular light surrounding the top portion of a large dark shape four times larger in diameter than the circular glow.

The UFO approached the base slowly and hovered. Now they could make out a second dimmer light on the bottom of the shadowy shape.

The object moved off to the east—disappeared. Then reappeared for a few seconds, disappeared again and then came back for a third time.

The tower operators called a radar site and were told that the UFO was on their scopes. The object was tracked by radar for about five minutes as it moved back and forth across Tokyo Bay.

An F-94 jet from Johnson Air Force Base was sent up just after midnight to get a good look at it if possible, and managed to close in near enough to get a radar fix on it for a minute and a half. Then the UFO pulled away fast!

Shortly afterwards both ground radar and the tower operators picked up the UFO again.

Two minutes later the UFO separated into three parts spaced about a quarter of a mile from each other, and raced from the area at high speed!

The late Edward J. Ruppelt in his book, *The Report on Unidentified Flying Objects,* had this to say about it: "I could go into a long discourse on the possible explanations for this sighting; I heard many, but in the end there would be only one positive answer—the UFO could not be identified as something we knew about. It could have been an interplanetary spaceship. Many people thought this was the answer and were all for sticking their necks out and establishing a category of conclusions for UFO reports and labelling it spacecraft. But the majority ruled and it remained an *unidentified* flying object."[7]

1952

OLORON AND GAILLAC, FRANCE

On October 17, 1952, the citizens of Oloron got a good look at a long cylindrically shaped spaceliner that they'll never forget. The large craft was blunt at both ends and tilted at a forty-five degree angle as it traveled slowly in a southwesterly direction.

Some fifteen pairs of flying saucers were observed to zig-zag back and forth rapidly ahead of the large craft, and from time to time when one member of a pair would draw away sharply from the other, a contrail was produced between them. The whole procession was a fantastic sight and was witnessed by numerous people, including the general superintendent of the Oloron High School, Monsieur Yves Prigent, and his family.

Ten days later, on October 27, a repeat performance was given, this time for the benefit of the citizens of Gaillac. Once again, the long tubelike space ship tilted at a forty-five degree angle, escorted by numerous pairs of saucers moving in zig-zag fashion and traveling in a southwesterly direction went through exactly the same scene as they had played at Oloron! At Gaillac the spacecraft were witnessed by about a hundred people.

There were two other items of interest in connection with these sightings:

(1) The spaceliner's propulsion system produced what was described as a white 'cottony cloud' beneath it.

(2) All of the craft shed a gossamer-like substance over the entire neighboring countryside which disappeared as fast as people tried to pick it up. This is a common characteristic of many saucers and the substance has been given the name of 'Angel Hair' among saucer researchers. We will be discussing this strange substance in a later chapter. As far as is known no one, either at Oloron or Gaillac, succeeded in retrieving any of the material for scientific analysis. It dissolved too quickly.[11]

Postscript to 1952 . . .

This was a vintage year for sightings both in quality and in quantity. On July 2, US Navy Chief Photographer, Warrant Officer Delbert C. Newhouse, took a color film of a fleet of flying saucers near Trementon, Utah.[12]

On July 14, Pan American Airlines pilot Captain William B. Nash and co-pilot Captain Fortenberry, flying at about 8,000 feet near Newport News, Virginia, at 8:15 P.M., sighted six large discs flying in echelon below their DC-4 at an estimated 12,000 m.p.h., but suddenly reversing direction on being joined by two more.[12]

Then, on both the nights of July 19-20 and 26-27 numerous UFOs gathered over Washington National Airport and Andrews Air Force Base (now renamed Edwards Air Force Base). Radar showed them moving off at high speed when jet interceptors approached.

Later, they returned after the jets had gone. The Washington sightings received tremendous publicity on the front pages of the US press.[12]

IV

1953

THE WEST MALLING AFFAIR

THE SCENE now shifts to England. At 10 A.M. on November 3, 1953, Flying Officer T. S. Johnson and his navigator, Flying Officer G. Smythe, were engaged in a reconnaissance flight in a Vampire jet night fighter.

They were at 20,000 feet when they spotted an object in the sky at a much higher altitude. At first glance the object seemed to be a bright star. However, a few seconds later the UFO suddenly buzzed them, passing straight over their jet at tremendous speed. Both airmen noticed that the craft was circular, and that a bright light wreathed its outer rim. The sighting lasted about half a minute.

When they landed at West Malling, Kent, the station commander, Group Captain P. H. Hamley after hearing their story sent a report to Fighter Command. They questioned the two airmen for an hour and a half.

The late Waveney Girvan in his book *Flying Saucers and Commonsense*,[13] pointed out that nine days elapsed before the War Office released further information to the effect that on the same day at 2:30 P.M. while a radar set was being tested at Lee Green, Kent, the scope locked on to a circular object that remained stationary for a long time before beginning to move off slowly until it passed beyond tracking range around 3:10 P.M. Presumably it was the same craft encountered by Messrs. Johnson and Smythe earlier in the day, or another just like it.

At any rate, from 2:45 P.M. to 3:10 P.M. it was observed by Mr. A. J. Jeffrey, technical storeman; D. Fuller, fitter mechanic; S. Russell, electrical control equipment, anti-aircraft group workshop; and H. Waller, sergeant radar operator. Sergeant Waller stated that the object they had all seen was quite definitly not a balloon. Furthermore, he added that this was not the first time he had seen strange objects on the radarscopes. He referred to an occasion when he had seen five objects flying in perfect formation much faster than any speed our aircraft are capable of. The War Office also stated *there had been three other trackings of a similar object between September 14 and 22.*

What was the sequel? On November 24 Mr. Birch, then Parliamentary Secretary, Minister of Defense, speaking in the House of Commons in reply to Lt. Colonel Schofield (Conservative) and Mr. Bellenger (Labor), who asked about flying objects recently observed by airmen and members of anti-aircraft command, said that two experimental meteorological balloons were observed at different times on November 3, and another by members of anti-aircraft command. There was nothing peculiar about either of the occurrences (laughter).

After further exchanges, Mr. Isaacs (Labor) asked: Will the Minister agree that this story of flying saucers is all ballooney? (loud laughter).

Mr. Birch said that Mr. Isaac's appreciation was very nearly correct (laughter).

Postscript to the West Malling Affair . . .

The London *Sunday Dispatch* on November 17, 1954, carried this sensational front-page headline, STRANGE SIGHTS IN SKY BAFFLE WAR OFFICE.[14]

Six times in the previous few weeks a strange pattern of 'blips' had appeared on inland radar screens in Britain. Neither the War Office which controlled inland radar, nor the Air Ministry could say what they were.

The 'blips' usually appeared about mid-day from no-where, flying at about 12,000 feet in an east to west direction. They would first be in a 'U,' or badly shaped hairpin formation. After a time they converged into parallel lines and then formed into 'Z' formation before disappearing.

The objects were invisible to the human eye, but on the radar screen their 'blips' represented forty and fifty echoes covering a wide area in the sky.

A War Office spokesman said they always followed the same pattern. He said they had checked and found their sets were not faulty. All their sets in the area had picked the objects up.

A *Sunday Dispatch* reporter spoke to one man who had seen them who affirmed he'd been issued very high-level orders to maintain utmost secrecy.

"And even if I did know what they are, I am too worried myself to say anything," he said.

The Air Ministry said there are many objects, such as meteorological balloons, experimental aircraft, carrier pigeons with metal rings on their legs and even toy kites, which could form an image on a radar screen.

However, radar operators know all about those things, and none of them causes such similar patterns as produced on six different days by the 'blips' in question.

Needless to say, both War Office and Air Ministry have remained strangely silent since these remarkable newspaper disclosures.

1954

THE CENTAURUS INCIDENT

The following is a fair sample of the sightings which occur rather frequently and is one of the best.

The time was just after sunset on June 29, 1954; the place, Labrador.

THE FLYING SAUCER STORY

A BOAC (Boeing Stratocruiser) *Centaurus* had taken off from Idlewild Airport at 5 P.M. New York time for London, Captain James Howard, one of BOAC's most experienced skippers was in command.

Dinner had been served on board and soon some of the passengers had gone to bed.

It was at 9:05 P.M. Labrador time that Captain Howard first sighted the UFOs. He observed that there was one big object with six smaller ones in attendance. He pointed them out to his co-pilot, First Officer Lee Boyd who flew with the famous Pathfinder Force during World War II. Lee had already spotted them.

The objects were about five miles off from the *Centaurus*, lined out parallel to their own line of flight. A big craft maintained center position while the smaller ones preceded and followed it 'fore and aft.'

These UFOs stayed parallel with the *Centaurus* for eighty miles. From time to time the big object changed shape, or appeared to do so—or possibly, as Captain Howard has suggested, altered its angle of flight giving the appearance of changing shape, and while this was going on the smaller objects changed their positions around it.

They checked with Goose Bay to see if any other formations of fighter aircraft or anything else was in the area and were given a negative reply. Goose Bay informed them they were sending a fighter up to investigate.

Meanwhile, the big object had changed shape from its original inverted pear-shape to what looked like a flying arrow. It seemed to be closing in on them but it didn't. Instead, it changed its appearance again until it resembled a giant telephone receiver the size of an ocean liner.

By this time in addition to the skipper and Lee Boyd, other members of the crew were observing the objects. George Allen, navigating officer; Douglas Cox, radio officer; Dan Godfrey, engineering officer, and Bill Stewart, the other engineering officer who was also a veteran flyer. Additionally, Daphne Webster, the stewardess, also saw the UFOs and said afterwards: "I have been flying for two years and have never seen anything like it before."

Just before the jet interceptor arrived on the scene the objects began to disappear. Captain Howard asked what had happened to the smaller ones. According to George Allen who had been watching them the whole time "it looked to me as though they went inside the big one."

Captain Howard related that he told the incoming jet pilot over the radio of their gradual disappearance culminating in the departure of the large object at tremendous speed.

Altogether, a crew of eight, plus fourteen out of his fifty-one passengers saw the objects which remained in parallel flight positions with the *Centaurus* accompanying them for eighteen minutes over a distance of eighty miles.

Captain Howard wrote in the December 11, 1954 issue of *Everybody's Weekly*,[15] "It was a solid thing. I'm sure of that, maneuverable and controlled intelligently— a sort of base ship linked somehow with those smaller attendant satellites.

"There is no rational explanation—except on the basis of space ships and flying saucers. On that basis it must have been some weird form of space ship from another world.

"If so, then another world was watching the *Centaurus* as it flew over Labrador that night in June—watching, waiting maybe. For what? One day we shall know and that day, I'm sure, will be pretty important for the human race. I hope I'm here to see it."

Incidentally, Captain Howard is now a senior pilot with BOAC flying VC-10s.

1955

IT PUT THE AIRPORT LIGHTS OUT!

On July 26, 1955, a brilliant circular UFO with a trail four or five times its own length flew in to Washington National Airport. It stopped and hovered, then began moving in an oscillatory configuration and eventually took off at high speed. However, it was caught in the beam of a searchlight from the airport, but suddenly the searchlight went out!

The UFO also caused the ceiling lights at the airport to go out, but these lit up again the moment the UFO left the airport.[3]

Postscript to 1955 . . . -

The following English sighting is mentioned here because it happened on the same day and is quoted here from *Flying Saucer Review.*[16]

"As Philip Wills, Britain's gliding champion, circled beneath a thermal cloud over Lasham airfield, Hampshire, during the National Gliding Championships, a boomerang-shaped object was spotted hovering over him by officials of the meeting.

"Dark, and thought to be about 3,000 ft. up, it was reported to the Air Ministry as being on a bearing of 290 degrees from Lasham airfield at an elevation of about 60 degrees. It hovered for about thirty seconds and then made off in a northwesterly direction at high speed. The Air Ministry later asked for further details.

"This incident is pretty well known now. It appeared in the press of the most Commonwealth countries; but for the record, the object was estimated at measuring about 40 ft. from tip to tip."

1956

HUGE SAUCER OVER PARIS

It was 10:50 P.M. on the evening of February 19, 1956. Bitterly cold but a clear night.

Inside the radar control room at Orly airport, Paris, an operator watched the scope. Suddenly, a 'blip' with a difference showed up with an 'echo' twice as large as that of the largest known aircraft. Furthermore, it behaved quite unlike anything the operator had ever seen before.[17]

The object would slow down, hover, then accelerate to fantastic speeds for a while.

Then a more familiar 'blip' appeared on the screen. This was soon recognized as an Air France Douglas Dakota airliner on the regular Paris-London service.

Orly radioed the pilot that a UFO was on its approximate path. Radio Officer Beaupertuis caught a glimpse of the object on the starboard beam through a porthole as he passed the message to the skipper. It was enormous, rather indistinct in outline, but here and there lit by a red glow.

The skipper, Captain Desavoi, made a report to the French Ministry of Civil Aviation. He said that they had watched the UFO for a full half minute. It was certainly no civil airliner for it carried none of the regular navigation lights.

The captain added that he was warned by Orly that the object had moved to his port side. Ten minutes later they called again advising the UFO was now several miles above the airliner but the crew did not see it again.

The radarmen at Orly Airport followed the UFO's fantastic flight over a radius of thirty minutes for four hours but the strange thing is that neither Le Bourget nor Paris Observatory picked it up on their radar screens.

Does this indicate that the flying saucers can choose where they want to be seen over certain areas?

1957

PORTUGUESE AIR FORCE SEES THEM

At 7:21 P.M. on the night of September 4, 1957, a flight of four jet fighter-bombers took off from Ota Air Base, Portugal. The aircraft were under the command of Captain Jose Lemos Ferreira and the pilots of the other planes were Sergeants Alberto Gomes Covas, Salvador Alberto Oliveira and Manuel Neves Marcelino.

The mission was a routine practice night navigation flight at 25,000 feet between Ota Air Base, the Spanish town of Granada, the Portuguese town of Portalegre and finally, to the Portuguese village of Coruche. It was a clear night and there was almost a full moon. The first leg of the flight to Granada went as scheduled and then they started a port turn to change course to Portalegre.

It was then that Captain Ferreira noticed an unusual light above the horizon on his port beam. After watching it closely for three or four minutes he alerted the other pilots to what he'd seen. The pilot on his right wing had already observed it. A radio discussion about the light ensued.

The object looked like a very bright star, unusually big and scintillating with a colored nucleus which changed color constantly, going from deep green to blue and then passing through yellowish and reddish colors-of the spectrum.

Suddenly, the object enlarged becoming according to Captain Ferreira's account, five or six times its initial size. Before the pilots had time to get over that spectacle the object shrank becoming a barely visible, small yellow point.

These expansions and contractions happened several times. The relative position between the aircraft and the object was still the same, that is, about forty degrees on their left. Captain Ferreira stated that they could not determine if the changing dimensions were due to very fast approaches and retreats on the same vector or if the changes took place while stationary. (Compare these comments with those of Captain Howard of the *Centaurus* as regards the constantly changing shape of the spaceliner he and his crew sighted in June 1954—Author). If the first explanation was correct the speed would be tremendous and far beyond the capabilities of our aircraft.

After about seven or eight minutes of these changes in size the object had been gradually getting down below the horizon and was now ninety degrees to their left.

Shortly before reaching the town of Portalegre at 10:38 P.M., Captain Ferreira decided to abandon their mission and make a port turn in the general direction of Coruche. In any case nobody was paying any attention to the exercise!

They turned about fifty degrees to port but still the object maintained its position of ninety degrees to their left which Captain Ferreira pointed out a stationary object couldn't do. By now the UFO had turned bright red and was well below their 25,000 feet altitude.

After several minutes on their new course the airmen spotted a small circle of yellow light coming out of the large object! Before they had time to get over that surprise the pilots noticed three other similar objects on the right of the main UFO.

The UFO and its attendant satellites were moving with their relative positions changing constantly and sometimes, very rapidly. Captain Ferreira stated that he still could not estimate how far away the UFOs were, although he realized that they were below them and very close.

In any case, the big object appeared to be ten to fifteen times greater in size than the smaller yellow ones and apparently was the director of operations since the others were moving around it.

The aircraft were now approaching Coruche. Suddenly, the lead spaceliner very rapidly made a dive and then soared upwards in a fast climb in their direction!

Then, Captain Ferreira reported, everyone went wild and almost broke formation in the process of getting across and ahead of the climbing UFO.

Captain Ferreira had quite a job calming his pilots down after this excitement. As soon as they had crossed over the path of the climbing UFO the objects began to disappear.

Their squadron landed without further incident after the most thrilling 'routine' flight of their careers. In all the episode had lasted forty minutes—time enough to come to some very definite conclusions.

They all agreed there was no rational explanation based on this everyday phenomena. Captain Ferreira stated: "After this please do not give us the old routine of Venus, balloons, aircraft and the like which has been given as a general panacea for almost every case of UFOs."

The Lisbon *Diario Illustrado*,[18] reported that the Coimbra Meteorological Observatory registered extraordinary variations on the magnetic field at the same time that Captain Ferreira and the other members of his flight were observing the space ships. This can be proved by diagrams at that establishment.

At the time of this sighting I was editor of *Flying Saucer Review*, which incidentally is now in its twelfth year of publication. The *Diario Illustrado* was the only Portuguese newspaper to publish an account of this amazing sighting. When a clipping reached the *Review* I immediately contacted our Lisbon correspondent, Senor D. Alves.

Senor Alves, who also writes for the Portuguese press, at once telephoned Captain Ferreira and was granted an interview at Ota Air Base. Furthermore, he was successful in obtaining a signed account from the flight commander, together with photographs of the captain and his three sergeant pilots. This account, together with the photographs appeared in the May-June 1958, issue of *Flying Saucer Review*. In its way, this was quite a scoop, especially as it has become increasingly difficult to get military pilots to discuss any encounters with UFOs.

I would like to take this opportunity to publicly thank Senor Alves for his prompt action, and Captain Ferreira and his fellow aviators for their courage in allowing this story to reach a wide audience.[19]

Postscript to 1957 . . .

1957 along with 1952 were vintage years, for saucer sightings snowballed on a world-wide scale immediately after Sputnik II was launched.

On November 5 the coastguard cutter *Sebago* tracked a UFO on radar over the Gulf of Mexico.[20]

Early in December a saucer with tripod undercarriage was claimed to be photographed at San Pedro by Radio Officer T. Fogl, a member of the crew of the British steamer *SS Ramsay*. The pictures he took were accepted for some years and published in many responsible journals including *Flying Saucer Review, Life* magazine, *The Illustrated London News*, and indeed, the first impression of this book. Finally after nearly ten years, on Mr. Fogl's own admission the pictures are now recognized as fakes. All this goes to show how very careful we must be in evaluating flying saucer photographs.

— V

1958

THE TRINIDAD ISLAND SAUCER

SHORTLY AFTER noon on January 16, 1958, a Brazilian Naval survey ship, the *Almirante Saldanha* participating in International Geophysical Year projects was preparing to cast off from the island of Trinidad which lies just off the coast of Brazil.

The ship's complement included a retired Brazilian Air Force officer, Captain Jose Teobalde Viegas, and, at the request of the Brazilian Navy, the expert underwater photographer Almiro Barauna, several other scientists, and a highly trained group of marine explorers.

Captain Viegas was on deck with several of the scientists and members of the crew, when a 'Saturn-shaped object' suddenly arrived upon the scene. They all spotted the UFO simultaneously. It came in over the island from the east, flew straight to Desejado Peak where it made an abrupt turn and sped off heading now on an east by northeasterly course.

At first sight of the object they shouted to Barauna below who grabbed up his camera and dashed up on deck. He managed despite the excitement to take excellent pictures of it.

After exhaustive analyses of the pictures and negatives by both the Navy Photo Reconnaissance Laboratory and the Cruzeiro de Sul Aerophotogrammetric Service they were cleared as absolutely genuine and the President of Brazil added his approval.

These, together with the story, made front page news in Rio de Janeiro's *Correio da Manha* on February 21.[22]

Four days later the United Press (Rio de Janeiro) carried the story asserting that the Brazilian Navy Ministry stood behind the authenticity of the UFO pictures, which were then released internationally.[23]

These photographs remain among the best ever taken of flying saucers. Who can doubt the existence of UFOs now?

1959

HAWAII

On Saturday, July 11, 1959, the crews of five different commercial airliners reported seeing a formation of UFOs about 1,000 miles east of Honolulu.[32]

Captain George Wilson, Pan American Airways, who was flying from San Francisco to Honolulu, said: "At 3:02 A.M. Hawaii time I saw one intensely bright light followed by four smaller ones. We were cruising at 20,000 feet with low clouds decked below us when the object first appeared about 1,000 feet above us and to our left.

"My co-pilot, Richard Lorenzen, of Los Altos, California, and flight engineer Robert Scott, stared open-mouthed as the light came towards us at an extremely high rate of speed.

"For at least ten seconds it maintained its course which was on an opposite heading to us; and had it been another aircraft it would have passed well to our left.

"Suddenly, the object made a sharp turn at a speed inconceivable to any vehicle we know and the light suddenly disappeared. The smaller lights were evenly spaced and were either a part of the mysterious object, or this was an example of darned good formation flying."

Captain Wilson discounted any possibility that the lights were any sort of reflection. "It was pitch dark," he said, "a total of five planes sighted the same object. It is absolutely impossible that it could have been a reflection."

When he landed in Honolulu Captain Wilson said he had never seen anything like this in his nineteen years of flying. He added that he had never believed such foreign objects existed.

"I'm a believer now," he said.

The other pilots who filed reports were Captain Lloyd Moffat, of Canadian Pacific Airways; First Officer Erwin Zedwick, of Slick Airways; Captain Noble Sprunger, of Pan American Airways, and Captain E. G. Kelley, also of Pan American.

Captain Moffat confirmed Captain Wilson's story. He said: "You can take it from me they were there. I never saw anything like it in my life and there are five of us who saw the same thing at the same time."

A US Air Force spokesman said that all the pilots filled out questionnaires and were interrogated about the sightings. The reports were then forwarded to Pacific Air Command in Honolulu, to the North American Defense Command and to Washington.

This remarkable sighting was reported widely by Associated Press, United Press International and Hawaiian newspapers.[24]

1960

THE MYSTERY SATELLITES

On February 11, 1960, various British newspapers and also the BBC Home Service carried reports from their New York or Washington representatives about a US Defense Department announcement that an unidentified object, then orbiting the Earth, had been discovered by a navy-operated space surveillance unit (i.e. by long-range radar) and was being kept under constant observation.[25][26][27]

The object was, the reports said, roughly orbiting the poles. It had so far preserved total radio silence and was of monster size about fifteen tons in weight. In their statement the US Department of Defense were careful to emphasize that the object "may have been of Soviet origin."

However, the same afternoon Professor Alla Masewich, the Soviet woman astronomer who was then in charge of seventy sputnik tracking stations said she "very much doubted" if it could be a Russian satellite. All Soviet Earth satellites, she said, had been fired into orbits of sixty-five degrees to the equator—taking them well clear of the poles. Her final and definite comment was: "If it was anything so useful as a satellite I would have expected to know about it. But this is the first I have heard of it."

Some months later on September 3, the London *Daily Telegraph*[28] reported on its front page the following:

"A mysterious space object which has appeared in the sky over New York five times since August 23 has been photographed by a tracking camera at the Grumman Aircraft Plant at Bethpage, Long Island. Its speed is thought to be about three times that of the Satellite Echo I. A spokesman for Grummans said the object was photographed at 8:50 P.M. last Thursday as it passed over the company's plant in a westerly direction. The announcement followed reports that scientists had detected an object of similar description over Chicago and various East Coast areas late last week. Observers said the object seemed to glow with an intermittent reddish light. It travels from east to west rather than the west to east path followed by man-made satellites."

There have been reports of mystery satellites in orbit around the Earth for some years now. Major Donald E. Keyhoe, US Marine Corps (Retd.), related in his book *The Flying Saucer Conspiracy*[29] how he'd learned that Professor Clyde Tombaugh was commissioned by the US Government to search for and confirm or not the presence of two satellites orbiting the Earth.

Postscript to 1960 . . .

A triangular UFO was sighted on May 22, 1960, at 9:33 A.M. by the Palma Observatory, Majorca. It appeared to be about one quarter the size of the moon and was spinning on its axis while proceeding on a steady course.[3]

1961

UFO OVER EXETER

The London *Evening News* for June 19, 1961[30] reported that a mystery object had been hovering stationary over Exeter Airport for some considerable time. Other reports mentioned that it could be seen for well over an hour. An official said: "It's been seen on radar northeast of Falmouth and we have had it under observation for some time but we still do not know what it is. We think it is at about 50,000 feet. It's shining brightly and appears to be pretty big." The airport was inundated with calls from people who had seen it.

When the Air Ministry was asked by the newspapers for an explanation they offered the balloon theory and suggested that it might have been released by Bristol University. The *Daily Mail* jumped at this explanation stating that "sky-hook balloons are launched from Bristol University to radio back soundings from the air." Other papers followed like sheep and another sighting was all but buried.

The *Flying Saucer Review*,[31] however, telephoned Bristol University and was told that they had not released such a balloon for over a year—a fact that any of the newspapers could have discovered for themselves.

There was also another reason why the mystery object could not have been a balloon launched from Bristol and reference to the wind and weather charts for June 19 all disclose that the wind was blowing steadily from the west during the whole period of the observation. If it had been a balloon it would have to be launched from America, in which case it wouldn't have reached Exeter. How could it have remained stationary for over an hour in the face of fifteen mile an hour winds?

Postscript to 1961 ...

The *Melbourne Sun*[32] reported that twelve round flying objects—moving fast in pairs—were sighted by ten independent witnesses near Meekartharra on August 14. Meekatharra is 480 miles northeast of Perth, Australia. The objects left a white trail of 'streamers' which floated to the ground—fine mesh-like streamers that crumbled and disappeared when picked up by the startled watchers at Mt. Hale Station, which is seventy-five miles distant from Meekatharra!

Shearing contractor Edwin Payne reported, "They were flying at 8,000 to 10,000 feet about the same speed as the Russian sputnik we saw a couple of years ago." He also remarked, "I picked up one of the streamers but it vanished in my hands as it touched my skin." Nothing daunted he drove back to the station again to see if he could find any streamers that wouldn't disappear—the object being to preserve them for analysis. His mission was not successful.

When the incident was reported to the police, Constable Jim Coyle checked with the Department of Civil Aviation and was told that there were no aircraft or meteorological balloons over the area at that time.

An official of the Royal Australian Air Force promised to make a report on the incident to the Department of Air. He even went so far as to say that the sighting was *very interesting.*

1962

SCHOOLBOY SNAPS SAUCERS

Some of the best flying saucer photographs have been taken by schoolboys. An example that comes to mind is the Stephen Darbishire photograph of an Adamski type saucer snapped on February 15, 1954, at Coniston, England.

Early in 1962, fourteen-year-old Alec Birch was taking snapshots of his dog in the back garden of his home at Mosborough, near Sheffield. Two young friends, David Brownlow, aged 12, and Stuart Dixon, aged 16, were both with him in the garden. [33] [34] [35] [36] [37] [38]

Suddenly, they noticed five dark objects above them in the sky. They were absolutely silent and not moving —just hovering up there.

Alec later described what happened at a meeting of the British UFO Association in London. He said:

"We stood looking at them, puzzling out what they could be. I think it was for about four seconds, when suddenly there appeared dazzling balls or blobs of light from the region of the objects, which seemed to dim. Then other blobs appeared, and the same thing repeated itself. I thought of my camera. It seemed as if seeing the lights urged me on to try and snap them which I promptly did. As I did so the lights seemed to dim and die away.

"Suddenly the objects seemed to move, as if gathering speed then shot off at a terrific rate in a northeasterly direction over Sheffield. There was no sound at any time."

The picture was not developed for some weeks and Alec Birch's family were amazed when they saw it showed five saucers—each with a small central dome—hovering above some trees.

The delay in getting the film developed caused some difficulty in pinpointing the actual date on which Alec took the picture. At first it was thought to have been in February but later Alec considered it more likely to have been on March 4.

The Alec Birch photograph and his story received considerable coverage in the *Yorkshire Post*,[39] *Sheffield Telegraph*,[40] and other newspapers. Additionally, the British Air Ministry investigated the sighting and Alec traveled to London and was interviewed at the Ministry. Subsequently, the Air Ministry gave it as their opinion that temperature inversions could have caused the effects which appeared on the photograph!

1963

THE YEAR OF THE CRATERS

During 1963 flying saucers continued to be reported from all over the world, but in Britain they took on a new significance. Mysterious craters started appearing in widely separated parts of the country indicating the possibility that a series of landings had taken place.[41] [42] [43] [44] [45]

The one that got most publicity in the press and on television was the Charlton crater in Wiltshire. It should be noted that just prior to the appearance of this crater there had been sighting reports in the neighborhood.

On July 16, the news broke that a farmworker, Reg Alexander, on Mr. Roy Blanchard's Manor Farm at Charlton, Wiltshire, had discovered a mysterious depression in a field where potato and barley crops were thriving. On the spot where the crater had suddenly appeared all trace of the crops had vanished. The depression was saucer-shaped, eight feet in diameter and about four inches in depth. In the center was a three foot hole variously described as from five inches to one foot in diameter with four slot marks (four feet long and one foot wide) extending out from the hole.

Mr. Blanchard sent for the police, who in turn, brought in the Army, and Captain John Rogers, chief of the Army Bomb Disposal Unit, of Horsham, Sussex, arrived to conduct investigations.

At that time Mr. Blanchard stated again there wasn't a trace left of the potatoes and barley that had been growing before the crater appeared. "No stalks, no leaves, no roots," and he added, "the thing was heavy enough to crush rocks and stones to powder. We heard no crash and whatever power it used produced no heat and no noise. I believe we have received a visit from a spaceship from another world."

Subsequently, the astronomer, Patrick Moore, visited the crater and pronounced that the object which had caused the depression was a meteorite. However, this explanation was eventually destroyed by Dr. F. G. F. Claringbull, Keeper of the Department of Mineralogy at the British Museum who made the significant remark, "There is more in this than meets the eye."[46]

This was by no means all. Craters had mysteriously appeared at Middle Moneynut, East Lothian, Scotland; Dufton Fell, Westmorland; Flamborough Head, Yorkshire; Southerness, Kirkcudbright, Scotland; and at Southampton.

Accounts of these other craters have appeared in the local press. Some of them, notably the ones at Meldon Hill, part of Dufton Fell, Westmorland, were truly gigantic in size, compared with the one at Charlton.

It would appear that saucer sightings were recorded in the vicinity of all these places just before or around the time these craters were discovered.

1964

THE SOCORRO AFFAIR

About 5:30 P.M. on April 24, 1964, Lonnie Zamora, a Socorro, New Mexico, police officer, was chasing a speeding motorist when he heard an explosion from the direction where a dynamite shack was located. Abandoning the chase, he turned the patrol car around and set off for the shed.

His first view as he approached the area mistakenly revealed what he thought was an overturned car; however, upon pulling up close he was amazed to see a smooth metallic egg-shaped object with the markings reproduced below (insignia of some sort) over a foot high painted in red on one side of the craft. [47] [48] [49]

At this point, his attention was drawn to two small figures dressed in what looked like white overalls that completely covered them from head to foot—hands and all.

Zamora got out of his car and walked towards them. Suddenly, the UFO began to roar emitting flames and smoke from beneath it.

Badly scared, he ran back and took cover behind his patrol car. He said, "I thought it was going to blow up!"

Then, all was quiet. "You could have heard a pin

drop." The UFO rose about ten feet without any further noise—just high enough to clear the eight foot dynamite shack by about two feet, and proceeded to skim along at a very low altitude for a mile or so before soaring up and on its way into the sky.

Zamora had put out a radio call for assistance the moment he spotted what he'd mistaken for an over- turned car. Therefore, he was joined shortly by State Police Sergeant Sam Chavez, but not before the craft had left the scene.

Together they approached the landing site where scorched ground and burned weeds were very much in evidence. They also found five rectangular depressions with a wedge-shaped cross section. Each depression was twelve inches long, ¼ of an inch wide and several inches deep. There were also some marks that were described by a sightseer as looking like the paw marks of a moun- tain lion.

Thirty-six hours later, around 12:30 A.M. on April 26, there was another UFO landing reported near La Madera, New Mexico, about 100 miles north of Socorro.

Orlando Gallegos told State Police he had spotted an object only 300 feet from his house that looked like a 'butane tank' emitting bluish-white flames. He watched it for a minute or so before the flames suddenly went out and the object disappeared.

Police Captain Martin E. Vigil and Officer Albert Vega investigated the case. Four depressions were found on the ground approximately eight by twelve inches, three or four inches deep and V-shaped at the bottom.

Postscript to the Socorro Affair ...

It was on April 24, around 10 A.M. that a craft meas- uring twenty feet long, twelve to fifteen feet wide, and about four feet thick with rounded ends (reminding one again of the 'butane tank'), paid a visit to Gary Wilcox's farm in Newark Valley, New York.

At that time, this young man was trying to work a 300-acre farm alone without benefit of ultra-modern aids —a nearly impossible feat. Needless to say, there was no time whatsoever for fun and games.

He had been spreading manure on a field lying quite some distance from his farm buildings, when he decided to walk down and take a look at the moisture condition of an adjoining field. He remarked later that as he walked into it "a funny feeling came over me that something was going to happen." No sooner had that registered when his eye caught a silvery flash, as though it might have been the sun glinting off an old ice chest that hadn't yet been removed from the field. Yet, that didn't make any sense. Then, the craft suddenly materialized before him out of thin air, and two figures about four feet high dropped to the ground from beneath it. Again, both were completely clad in silvery one-piece suits—no facial features visible.

One of the visitors approached him while the other remained close to the craft. Both held trays in their arms heaped with soil samples—no hands or fingers visible. After assuring him there was no need for alarm, a lengthy conversation ensued.

They asked many naive questions from Wilcox's viewpoint about the chemistry of fertilizers, and in return gave him much information about space science and mechanics that was way over his head as space had hardly been a concern of his. They said they'd come from Mars, but unfortunately Gary didn't think to ask where they'd come from *before* dropping in on Mars, as anyone (including a well-programmed robot) would be highly interested in the soil created by a planet's electromagnetic generator as opposed to one that had none at all.

They told him that changes would occur in the Universe (not galaxy) which would inevitably have an effect on this solar system. That Mars might some day take up the position now occupied by Earth.

In addition, they also asked if they might have a sample of the chemical fertilizer that Wilcox had mentioned. This, he duly deposited in the field long after they had disappeared noiselessly into thin air. The bag of fertilizer was gone the following day.

One other curious thing in connection with their sudden materialization and dematerialization was their concern about having been observed at all, as they said they shouldn't have been visible beyond 100 feet (this type of craft apparently deflects light rays) and they prefer to utilize this mechanism daytimes rather than be spotted by the glow their craft gives off at night.[50] [51]

1965

CHALAC

The following report from the newspaper *Cordoba*,[52] published in the city of that name, was sent to *Flying Saucer Review* by its Argentine correspondent, Senor Oscar A. Galindez. The newspaper report was translated by Gordon Creighton, consultant and contributor to the *Review*, and contained in an article by him.[53]

"A fantastic thing occurred last Sunday at Chalac, near Formosa, on the Argentine-Paraguay frontier. Several saucers flew around for a while and then one of them landed. The local populace, consisting of some fifty South American Indians of the Toba tribe, stood rooted to the spot in amazement, and when three beings enveloped in 'luminous halos' emerged from the machine, the Indians went down on their knees before them with arms uplifted in the traditional manner of salutation used by their sun-worshipping ancestors when greeting the Sun, Lord of the World, Giver of Life.

"The three beings came towards them very slowly, either because they found the terrain difficult, or perhaps, because of some difficulty with our atmosphere.

"An Indian made to approach the saucer, but was dissuaded by one of the visitors, who, with friendly gestures, indicated that he should keep away from the craft. Then suddenly, the Indians began to hear a voice coming from one of the visitors, urging them to remain calm, for there was nothing to fear. They would never forget what they were now seeing, the voice continued, for the Space People would return in order to convince Earth men of their existence and to bring to this world the peace that it so badly needs.

"Then the Space Beings returned slowly to their machine, all the time bathed in luminous beams emanating from the craft. The saucer then took off, and its luminosity was now so great that the Indians were blinded by it.

"And so a humble community of the peaceful Toba Indians—perhaps more 'open' to such things than harassed city dwellers beset by material cares—have had the privilege of experiencing a cosmic visit which will have expanded their capacity for understanding.

"Photographs of the machine, taken by the local Argentine police authorities, provide a total refutation of any possible doubts as to the existence of these craft from other worlds, and a record of the most sensational occurrence of our times."

Postscript to 1965 . . .

Many sightings and landings were reported all over the world during 1965, though the South American scene seemed to have the bulk of the activity, including the sensational sighting of a UFO which hovered over Bahia Blanca for a considerable time. Some good photos of this saucer were taken and published in Buenos Aires newspapers.[54]

Three Japanese pilots reported that they encountered a UFO on the evening of March 18. This occurred during flights between Hiroshima and Osaka. Mr. Yoshiaka Inaba, pilot of Toa Airlines, was flying a Convair 240 with forty passengers aboard over Himeji City when he contacted the UFO. It kept pace with his plane for three minutes. He said the object emitted a greenish colored light. His co-pilot was Mr. Majima. The third pilot was Mr. Negishi flying a Tokyo Airlines small aircraft, a Piper Cherokee 140, who met up with a reddish white UFO which approached from behind his plane ten miles east of Takamatsu City. It then vanished out of sight at incredible speed.[55][56][57][58][59]

An oval-shaped object landed at 5:45 A.M. in a lavender field in the Basses-Alps in the South of France on June 29. The farmer, Monsieur Masse, was up early. It is hot at that time of the year in that part of France and no doubt work is done early in the day. He heard a noise something like that made by a helicopter and then suddenly saw the object in his field. A little man was near the machine dressed in what appeared to be some kind of one-piece space suit.

When the visitor saw the farmer he immediately got back into the machine which was evidently a very small one and took off. However, the farmer was able to note that there was a second occupant of the saucer, inside the vehicle, similarly attired.

Monsieur Masse is considered a person of good common sense and repute in the neighborhood. He called in the local *gendarmerie* and an investigation was begun. A depression was found where the saucer had landed and markings where the legs of the craft had embedded in the ground. Furthermore, although the soil in the area was sun-baked and hard, the spot where the saucer had landed was damp. Does not this indicate a sample was taken? There was also a hole in the middle like at Charlton, Wiltshire.[60][61][62]

Early in July a sensational and extremely well-authenticated sighting occurred in Antarctica. The Brazilian newspaper, *O Estado de Sao Paulo* gave the following report with a July 8 date-line:

"For the first time in history, an official communiqué has been published by a government about the 'Flying Saucers.' It is a document from the Argentine Navy, based on the statements of a large number of Argentine, Chilean and British sailors stationed in the naval base in Antarctica.

"The communiqué declares that the personnel of Deception Island naval base saw, at nineteen hours forty minutes on July 3, a flying object of lenticular shape, with a solid appearance and a coloring in which red and green prevailed, and, for a few moments, yellow. The machine was flying in a zig-zag fashion and in a generally western direction, but it changed course several times and changed speed, having an inclination of about forty-five degrees above the horizon. The craft also remained stationary, for about twenty minutes, at a height of approximately 5,000 metres, producing no sound.

"The communiqué states moreover that the prevailing meteorological conditions when the phenomenon was observed can be considered excellent for the region in question and the time of year. The sky was clear and quite a lot of stars were visible.

"The Secretariat of the Argentine Navy also states in its communiqué that the occurrence was witnessed by scientists of the three naval bases and that the facts described by these people agree completely. It is understood that the photographs taken by a photographer at one of these bases will be made public after they have been analyzed by scientists."[140]

1966

The London *Times* with a date-line from New York of March 22, stated that an investigation had been started into reports of a UFO, accompanied by four sister craft which about forty people had seen over a swamp at Ann Arbor, Michigan, U.S.A., on Sunday, March 20. The witnesses included twelve policemen and according to *The Times* their descriptions tallied.

Postscript to 1966 . . .
At the time of writing the year has hardly got under way, but it is only too apparent that the saucers are still with us. In England, newspaper reports have stated that a police officer observed a UFO in the Manchester area and many people in the Southend district have seen an object shaped like an ice cream cone. Reports have appeared in local papers.

VI

It was at the end of February 1962, that Colonel Glenn backed by the sound Mercury program and thousands of reliable, ingenious and brilliant personnel, became a household name and a much beloved astronaut due as much to his exceptional character and attitude as to his successful orbital flight around the Earth.

He was not alone in spirit (nor is any other astronaut, for that matter). The television world, which probably includes most of our readers, flew the mission with him and afterwards listened avidly to every word he had to say about the flight.

Although everyone will agree it was all very absorbing,

one particular item both puzzling and interesting stuck in the minds of people well versed in flying saucers. We refer, of course, to 'the little green fireflies.'

Colonel Glenn had reported back during the flight that the only unusual thing he'd seen so far were thousands of little luminous particles around the capsule, which he hadn't noticed till sunrise over the Pacific.

Later, when asked about it during his press conference, he said at first he thought he was looking into a complete starfield because there were literally thousands of them which he estimated were spaced six to ten feet apart giving the impression of looking into nothing but a starfield. "But this wasn't the case, because a lot of the little things that I thought initially were stars were actually bright yellowish-green about the size and intensity of looking at a firefly on a real dark night." Then he said: "They did not appear to emanate from the capsule."

Right here we get into some interesting scientific problems that plague space engineers:

(1) The difference between molecular action at sea level under atmospheric pressure of fifteen pounds per square inch, and that which occurs in 'free space' under near-vacuum conditions, or thin vacuum, if you prefer, as there is no such thing in nature as an absolute vacuum.

(2) The 'ultraclean' factor.

(3) Instant bonding.

What happens is this. Atmospheric pressure tends to keep molecules separated by virtue of putting 'slip covers' on them composed of dirt, moisture, oxides, etc. Ask any woman who keeps house whether it's possible to get any part of it absolutely clean and keep it that way, and she'll say "NO!" in letters two feet high. However, in space the exact opposite occurs. Here, all the natural film that can't be scrubbed away on Earth begins to peel off by the capsuleload (new word substitution for 'carload!').

Before we all shout together, "That's for me!" hold on—there's a catch! Along with nature's 'ultraclean-up' brigade, a molecular 'freeway' is born. What happens electromagnetically is all very complicated but the general idea is this. With nothing any longer separating the molecules they become magnetically attracted to each other—glued, if you like. The result? Instant bonding! It is no small feat upstairs to keep machinery operable.

So, with the sun shining through the dirt, it is almost certain these thousands of little particles would look like flickering yellowish-green fireflies, and we believe this is what Colonel Glenn and the other astronauts have seen and described from time to time.

The puzzling thing is, that since these space problems are known the world over and are not 'classified,' why haven't the astronauts told the public what the phenomenon was? Why were they not allowed to? It's as though everyone in the 'civilized' world today were obliged to follow a script in the same way an actor does. Drop your script and you're out of a job!

The second part of the puzzle involves the late George Adamski, a very controversial figure in flying saucer research, who—for those of you who haven't read about him—was the most publicized 'contactee' of modern times.

He claimed that he had a conversation with a pilot of a Venusian flying saucer at Desert Center, California, on November 20, 1952. There were six witnesses with him who watched from about half a mile away. (It was also included in his original account that military aircraft were flying and circling over the area at the time. I have a photostat letter on file from Project Blue Book which states emphatically that an Air Force pilot reported a UFO in the general vicinity of Desert Center, California, November 20, 1952. This, of course, does not prove that a saucer landed and contacted Adamski, but it does prove that a UFO or UFOs were in the area.)

Subsequently, Adamski claimed to have been taken for several rides in flying saucers, and also to have visited a big parent craft. He wrote books, lectured all over the world about his experiences, but was always the center of controversy even among those who believed in saucers.

However, in his book *Inside the Space Ships*,[63] he wrote—and mind you, this was eight years before Colonel Glenn's observations, "I was amazed to see that the background of space is totally dark. Yet there were manifestations taking place all around us, as though billions and billions of fireflies were flickering everywhere moving in all directions as fireflies do . . ." The similarity is remarkable, isn't it?

Now the puzzling things are these. Had Adamski really seen the 'fireflies' from a space ship, or had he been told about it by a friend who perhaps was a space scientist? The 'ultraclean' factor was not unknown to science even in those early years. However, there was something during those early years you couldn't say. You dared not speak of intersolar flight. If you had the courage to mention flying saucers at all, you had to say they were from Venus or Mars, or at least some planet in this little solar system of ours. The chances were you'd be thought a little less crazy if you did. So, were the craft Adamski saw and rode in products of his probing mind, or really of Venusian origin, or from this solar system at all?

The third part of the puzzle deals with what we've been calling 'magnetic shields' for nearly twenty years —shields that are generally around the craft keeping the structure molecularly unchanged and impervious to all matter outside them. (Gordon Evans has recently renamed it a 'gravity inertia screen,' which we think is far better and more descriptive.) With this screen in proper working condition there should be no particles peeling off the craft in space, and therefore no beautiful fireflies. Assuming Adamski did ride in these craft, were they the inferior models we mentioned earlier? Or had the craft landed, shut off the propulsion systems, picked up our atmospheric dirt and then peeled in space as all good little unprotected spacecraft do?

There's only one problem with that. Either it would have ruined the propulsion system and its screen, or ruined the shell of the craft. Why? Because these craft are famous for their seamless metal shells which we can't duplicate yet. Therefore, we know our space neighbors manufacture them in a vacuum. Remember, instant bonding? It would seem reasonable to assume one would take special care to protect the original molecular binding.

Probably one of the most intriguing things about Adamski's experiences is that we cannot recall a single instance when he stated his space friends shut off the propulsion mechanism, either to speak with him or to take him aboard.

Now we come to the fascinating case of Joe Walker, a test pilot employed since 1945 by the National Aeronautics and Space Administration (NASA). Walker took over the supersonic X-15 plane on March 25, 1960. Previously, the X-15 pilot had been Scott Crosfield, employed by the plane's manufacturers, the North American Aviation Company. All this information is important because in the light of what was to occur it is significant that Walker was employed by a US Government agency.

On May 11, 1962 pilot Joe Walker was lecturing at the Second National Conference on the Peaceful Uses of Space Research in Seattle, Washington, USA, and he stated:

"I don't feel like speculating about them. All I know

is what appeared on the film which was developed after the flight." (He was referring to objects caught by his camera during his record-breaking fifty-mile high flight in April.) They appeared to be cylindrical or discoid-shaped. There were five or six of them and Walker admitted *that this was the second occasion on which he had filmed UFOs in flight.*

This story was given some space in the London *Daily Telegraph*[64] and the *Daily Mail*[65] but in a very reduced form. However, the Paris *Le Matin*[66] added the highly significant detail that Joe Walker had also admitted that "it was one of his appointed tasks to detect these unidentified objects."

Flying Saucer Review[67] cabled NASA headquarters in California asking for further information and copies of the stills from the film taken by Walker's camera. The following cabled reply was received on May 22.

"Objects recently reported by NASA pilot Joe Walker have now been identified as ice flaking off X-15 aircraft. Analysis of additional film cameras mounted on top the X-15 led to identification of the previously unidentifiable objects. Ice forms on the X-15 after it is filled with liquid oxygen. No still photos are available. Lynn Manly Public Information Officer NASA Flight Research Center Edwards California."

The same explanation was also given immediately afterwards by the *Daily Telegraph*[68] with a Washington dateline. This caused Mr. Charles Gibbs-Smith, the well-known aeronautical historian and Keeper of Extension Services at the Victoria and Albert Museum, London, to telephone the newspaper. His remarks were carried by the Peterborough column. "For the love of Mike!" he protested, "what would they get on the lens at that speed and nearness?" (It must also be emphasized that heat not cold would be the problem at that height and speed.)

Another thing. It is also most interesting that the stills are no longer available. They were shown at Joe Walker's lecture but now are no more to be seen.

It would appear that Joe Walker had spoken out of turn and the authorities had to work overtime thinking up 'explanations' to salvage the situation. But had he, really? We think not. Trust a pilot not to drop his script these days. And trust administration to have thought up ridiculous explanations in advance. It all fits so perfectly into the dual policy, doesn't it?

The clincher is Major Robert White! On July 17, Major White piloted a X-15 experimental rocket to a height of fifty-eight miles, breaking the altitude record by eleven miles.

When he got back to earth he reported seeing a strange object in space at the top of his climb.

"I have no idea what it could be. It was grayish in color and about thirty to forty feet away."

Then, according to *Time Magazine*, Major White is reported to have said dramatically over his radio during the flight: "There *are* things out there. There absolutely is!"[70]

That did it! In the first place, Major White is a highly educated man, extremely articulate, an expert pilot who knows aero-space science as well as aerodynamics from A to Z. Like all others in this field, he knows the discoid design is aerodynamically perfect, and in accord with good flight principles. Left to himself uncoached, unprompted, there's not the slightest chance this brilliant man would refer to a circular model craft as a 'thing!'

The question is why should administration want such a craft referred to as a 'thing.' Certainly they know it's extraterrestrial in origin, far in advance of our technology, and the worst possible diplomacy to do so.

Semantics, word association, is the only answer that comes to mind. A number of years ago Hollywood ob-

liged by producing a ghastly (and insulting) horror
movie called *The Thing*. This miserably stupid film
about spaceships from other worlds has been played, re-
played again and again on television until by now it
must be threadbare. (In the USA it has often been run
in the children's 5 P.M. hour on TV.) Needless to say,
the astronauts are heroes to the children. Literally, they
couldn't be more 'glued' to the space program listening
to every word our astronauts say. Why do the authorities
want the coming generation to associate fear and horror with extraterrestrial spacecraft? There is no valid
or excusable reason for such a blatant diplomatic blunder.
The authorities should consider this matter carefully
and use the power of censorship where it is more ur-
gently needed, and lift it where it most certainly is not.

Major White's sighting in space does not conclude our
account of what astronauts have seen. During the twen-
tieth orbit of the earth by the Gemini IV space ship
crewed by astronauts James McDivitt and Ed White, a
remarkable incident occurred. They not only saw a UFO
in space but took pictures of it![71]

The London *Times*[72] reported:

"America's Gemini IV space ship sighted another
winged object hurtling along in space above the United
States this evening. It could not be immediately identified, although one official said it might be another satellite and Major James McDivitt, the Gemini commander,
reported that he had taken photographs of it."

The *Flying Saucer Review* reporting this happening,
quoted the above report and also that of the London
Daily Mirror[73] of the same day, as follows: "The discovery started frantic efforts by US Space experts to
track the object, and to guess its origin. A top official
said the paths of all orbiting objects were known, and
none of them was on a collision course with Gemini IV."

The strange thing is that the photograph does not
show any wings as mentioned by *The Times* in its report.

Yes, there are space ships out there and our astronauts will gradually become accustomed to seeing many more cruising on the oceans of space.

VII

MANY PEOPLE erroneously believe that the flying saucers are a modern phenomenon. This is far from being the case. The flying saucers have always been with us.

There are reports of strange flying objects in the skies going back through the centuries. They may well have been around for thousands of years, if we believe what the legends of pre-historic times tell us. There are records of them in the ancient Hindu Vedas where the craft are referred to as Vimanas. They were known in Ancient Egypt as you will see in the following pages. The Red Indians of North America tell of them in their folklore. However, let us start our trek back through history nearer to our own times.

1946

The year before Kenneth Arnold's sighting got such wide press coverage the tremendous post-war increase of visitations from extraterrestrial sources had already begun.

At about 6 P.M. on August 1, 1946, Captain Jack E. Puckett was flying a C-47 plane from Langley Field, Virginia, to MacDill Field, Florida.[3]

The aircraft was at 4,000 feet and about thirty miles northeast of Tampa when Captain Puckett and his crew were startled to see a cigar-shaped object hurtling towards them in horizontal flight at the same altitude.

When the cigar was about 1,000 yards distant it swerved to avoid them and as the UFO passed them the crew could see that the object was twice the size of a B-29 bomber and had luminous portholes.

In addition to Captain Puckett, both his co-pilot Lt. Henry and his engineer witnessed the object. When they landed a full report was given to the Base Operations Section of MacDill Field. A signed report from Captain Puckett's remarkable sighting is on file at NICAP Headquarters.

During the summer and autumn of that year the so-called 'ghost rockets' were seen over Sweden and Denmark. More than two thousand were reported and were cigar-shaped.

1945

During March 1945, fourteen men on the USAT *Delarof* in the area of the Aleutian Islands saw a dark spherical object rise out of the water. It circled their ship and flew off. An official report was sent to Washington.[3]

There have been many reports of strange objects entering and emerging from the seas as will be seen in a later section of this book.

1944

During World War II numerous pilots of both sides were tagged by luminous balls, which seemed to be intelligently controlled and to almost dance on the wing tips of their planes. These were called 'foo-fighters.'

On November 23, 1944 Lt. Edward Schluter of the US 415th Nightfighter Squadron saw eight to ten fiery balls flying in formation at tremendous speed. Other witnesses were Radar Officer Lt. Donald J. Meiers and Intelligence Officer Lt. F. Ringwald.[3][74]

One December night, the same year, a Major Leet, a bomber pilot, saw a luminous disk follow his plane and its maneuvers, while flying over Klangenfurt, Austria.[3]

1942

On February 26, 1942, the cruiser *Tromp*, of the Royal Netherlands Navy, was in the Timor Sea. Suddenly, a large aluminum disk flew towards the ship at tremendous speed. The UFO then circled high above the Dutch vessel for about three to four hours. Finally, it flew off at an estimated 3,000 to 3,500 m.p.h. The officer on duty was unable to identify it as any known aircraft.[75]

At midnight on March 25, the same year, Pilot Officer Roman Sobinski was returning from a bombing raid on Essen. While over the Zuider Zee, Holland, his tail gunner reported a round disk following their aircraft.

Sobinski saw that the object was closing in on his aircraft and gave instructions to fire on it. Several rounds appeared to enter the disk but made no impression. The object was of a luminous orange color. It appeared at 15,000 feet about 100 to 200 yards away. Its estimated speed was 180 m.p.h., but it disappeared at an estimated 1,000 m.p.h.[74]

1935

During the Ethiopian War in October, 1935, a disk-haped object hovered motionless in the sky above Adlis Ababa, Ethiopia, and was seen by many witnesses.[11]

1931

Mr. Francis Chichester, the famous yachtsman, well known for his lone crossings of the Atlantic, was in his earlier days an equally known airman who made many daring flights in his Moth plane.

In 1931, Mr. Chichester took off on a flight across the Tasman Sea from New South Wales, Australia, to New Zealand. He was alone in his tiny Moth airplane with an open cockpit.

There was nothing in the sky except for one or two clouds. Suddenly, he saw what looked like a dull gray-white airship approaching him. It was pearl-shaped, flashing brightly, periodically vanishing, re-appearing, accelerating and finally disappearing.[76]

1926

Nicholas Roerich, the well-known explorer and artist was traveling with his expedition in Mongolia. At 9:30 A.M. on August 5, 1926, Roerich and some members of his caravan were watching the flight of a black eagle when they caught sight of a huge oval-shaped object. It was flying far above the bird and had a shiny surface, one side of which was brilliant in the sun. It was moving at great speed from north to south. They watched it through binoculars and saw the shining craft while crossing their camp change its direction from south to southwest. Eventually, it disappeared in the blue sky.[77]

THE FLYING SAUCER STORY

—

1917

In 1917, while World War I was still being fought, six extraordinary sightings (which can also be classed as landings) took place around the village of Fatima, about sixty-two miles north of Lisbon, Portugal. At that time Portugal was a very backward country and illiterate peasants naturally put a religious connotation to the seemingly miraculous events that occurred.

The witnesses were: Lucia de Jesus, aged ten, and her cousins Francisco Marto and Jacinto Marto, aged nine and seven, as well as shepherds.

The fifth sighting had several hundred witnesses and the sixth, 70,000 witnesses.

On May 13, the children were collecting their sheep when there was a flash in the sky. A few minutes later a radiant figure appeared close to a small oak tree. To three illiterate children from a Catholic country fifty years ago this was the Holy Virgin. The radiant lady spoke to them telepathically.

The lady reappeared again on June 13, and this time she told the children she'd like them to learn to read.

The third contact was a month later. By this time many clergymen were not only skeptical but bitterly hostile and the local rector thought the Devil himself was tempting the children. In fact, the children were put in prison for a few days. At the third contact the radiant Lady said she would perform a miracle in October to convince everybody.

The fourth contact was to have taken place on August 13, but the children were interrogated and threatened by the Mayor of Vila Nova, Arturo d'Oliveira Santos. He then kidnapped and further threatened the children. Eventually they were released and met the

71

Being in an unexpected place—in the Valinnos (Little Valleys).

On September 13, the fifth contact took place and there were several hundred witnesses, including the Rev. General Vicar of Leira. According to him, the Lady came in an "airplane of light," an "immense globe, flying westwards at moderate speed. It irradiated a very bright light."

Other witnesses saw a white Being come out of the globe. The three children were again told by the Lady that She would perform a miracle in October. On this occasion 'Angel Hair'—a characteristic of many modern sightings—fell from the skies "as snowflakes" which melted away upon falling to the ground. After several minutes the globe took off and flew away in the direction of the sun.

The final sighting took place, as promised, on October 13, and was witnessed by 70,000 people, including reporters sent from Lisbon.

During the morning it had been raining hard, but at midday the rain slackened off to a drizzle as a great light shone through the clouds. The light began a fantastic dance, then rotated with increasing speed until it began falling towards the Earth. Many people felt heat from it and a prickling sensation.

Astronomical observatories everywhere had not noted anything unusual on that day, so the sighting at Fatima on October 13 was a local phenomenon bearing all the hallmarks of a giant flying saucer which put on a fantastic performance for 70,000 people.[78] [79] [80] [81] [82]

1916

At 11 P.M. on July 31, 1916, a bright object was seen hovering in the sky over Ballinasloe, Ireland.[83] It was visible for fifteen minutes before traveling to the north-west. It was then observed to hover for a further forty-five minutes. Then the UFO returned to where it was first noticed. Eventually, Venus, the morning star, rose on the horizon at 4 A.M., at which time the object vanished.

1909

The Encyclopaedia Britannica[84] states that from 1897 onwards Count Ferdinand von Zeppelin, of the German Army, was engaged in constructing an immense balloon, truly an airship. His first one was tested in June 1900, when it attained a speed of 18 m.p.h. and traveled a distance of three and a half miles before an accident to the steering caused the flight to be discontinued.

In 1905, Zeppelin built a second airship which after making some successful trips was wrecked in a violent gale, and then a third airship was produced which at its trials in October, 1906, traveled around Lake Constance.

Meanwhile, in 1901, Alberto-Santo Dumont had begun experiments in France with dirigible balloons. He was able to guide one from St. Cloud around the Eiffel Tower, Paris, and back in half an hour.

In October, 1907, the *Nulli Secundus,* an airship built for the British War Office, successfully journeyed from Farnsborough around St. Paul's Cathedral to the Crystal Palace, Sydenham—about fifty miles—in three hours thirty-five minutes.

That is the background to the early days of airships.

What then are we to make of the spate of reports of cigar-shaped objects seen over New Zealand in 1909?[85]

During a six-week period from the last week in July to the first week in September hundreds of eye-witnesses reported airships in the skies over New Zealand.

The objects were seen by residents in both North

Island and South Island. They were sighted both by day and by night.

1905

On February 1, a brilliant object was reported hanging motionless over Wales.[86]

During the same year, for several nights in succession a glowing disk with a corona was seen over Cherbourg, France.[86]

1904

On February 24, the SS *Supply* sighted three luminous disks which appeared from the ship to cover an area four times that of the sun. They were flying in formation first below some clouds, estimated at 5,000 feet. Then they climbed up into the cloud bank and disappeared.[83]

Nineteenth Century

1897

If we bear in mind the background to the early days of airships given earlier and also that although they were used in World War I their range was very restricted and they had difficulty in getting back to Germany after their raids over England, then we can well imagine that when a great black airship appeared over Kansas City, Missouri, in April 1897, it was a little before its time!

It was seen by 10,000 people. "Object appeared very swiftly, then appeared to stop and hover over the city for ten minutes at a time, then after flashing green-blue and white lights, shot upwards into space."[87]

There were many similar reports of a strange airship over the United States in April 1897. It was seen over the states of Illinois, Iowa, Michigan, Nebraska and Wisconsin.[83 84]

1883

On August 12, 1883, an astronomer called Bonilla at the Observatory of Zacatecas, Mexico, saw 143 circular objects crossing the sun obliquely to its poles. The next day more objects were seen crossing the solar disk. This must have been a veritable armada of celestial space-craft! Bonilla managed to obtain a photograph of one of the objects in the procession.[83 89]

During the same summer, according to a letter from Herr Blunk, of Hamburg, published in the West German magazine, Der Stern, "all the children and the teacher in the public school at Segeberg, saw in the sky two fiery balls, the size of full moons, traveling side by side, not very swiftly, from north to south, on a clear and sunny day."[9]

1880

On August 20, 1880, Monsieur Trecul, a member of the French Academy, observed a glittering white-gold cigar-shaped object with pointed ends. He also saw a smaller saucer leave the parent craft.[9]

1874

On July 6 at Oaxaca, Mexico, a huge, gently swaying, trumpet-shaped object estimated to be 425 feet long hovered in the sky for six minutes.[83]

1833

On November 13 a large, square, luminous craft was seen for more than an hour over Niagara Falls.[83]

1820

On September 7, 1820, a fantastic stream of flying saucers flying in perfect formation crossed the town of Embrun, France. While still maintaining precision formation they were seen to execute a perfect ninety degree turn and continue their flight on a new course.[83]

Eighteenth Century

1777

On June 17, 1777, the French astronomer Charles Messier, saw a number of dark round objects in the sky.[83]

1762

On August 9, 1762, a huge spindle-shaped object was seen crossing the sun by two different observatories in Switzerland. At Lausanne, Monsieur de Rostan observed this enormous craft *nearly every day for a month*. He managed to photograph it with his 'camera obscura' and sent the photograph (probably the earliest taken of a flying saucer) to the Academy of Sciences in Paris.

Monsieur de Coste at Sole, some distance from Lausanne, also focused an eleven-foot telescope on to the strange object.[9]

1741

On December 11, 1741, at 9:45 A.M. Lord Beauchamp was in Kensington Gardens, London. The sun was shining brightly. Suddenly, he noticed towards the south "a ball of fire, as it seemed, eight inches in diameter, but oval in shape" which "grew to the size of a yard and a half in diameter, and seemed to descend from above to about half a mile from the Earth. It went east and seemed to drop over Westminster. In its course it assumed a tail eighty yards long, and before disappearing it divided into two heads. It left a trail of smoke, all the way, and where it dropped, or seemed to drop, smoke ascended for twenty minutes, and at length formed into a cloud which assumed different colors."[9]

1718

Sir Hans Sloane, a famous physician, who was later to become President of the Royal Society, had a remarkable sighting of what we'd call today a UFO.

"A great light that suddenly appeared in the western sky, on March 19, 1718 at 7:45 P.M.," he stated.

"It shone with a brightness much greater than the Moon, which was then shining brightly. At first I thought it was only a rocket, but it *moved more slowly than a falling star in a direct line.* (Italics mine—Author.) It seemed to descend below the stars in the constellation of Orion. A long stream was branched in the middle, and the meteor turned pear-shape, or tapered upwards. At the lower end, it became spherical, but not so big as the full Moon. The color of it was white and blue, and the luster was dazzling, like the sun on a clear day. I had to turn my eyes from it, so bright was it. It moved about thirty seconds, and went out about twenty degrees below the horizon. Behind it, it left a track of faint red yellow, like glowing coals. It seemed to sparkle but *kept place without falling*. (Italics mine—Author.) I hear it was also seen at Oxford and Worcester."[9]

The Earlier Centuries

1686

The German astronomer, Gottfried Kirch, reported from Leipzig that on July 9, 1786, at 1:30 A.M. he observed "a burning globe, furnished with a tail, appearing apparently 8¼ degrees from Aquarius, and remained immovable for one eighth of an hour. Its diameter was about half that of the moon. It emitted so much light that at first one could read without a candle. Afterwards it vanished in its place, but very gradually."

Astronomer Kirch went on to state that the object had also been seen by others at the same time "and especially by Schlazius, at a city eleven miles away in Germany, from Leipzig."[82]

1619

A prefect of a Swiss Canton, Christopher Schere, saw a long, bright object flying along a lake, near Fluelen, Switzerland.[86]

1520

At Erfurt, Prussia, in the time of Emperor Carlos V, two burning suns were seen. Then a great "burning beam" landed suddenly. It took off again into the sky, where it became circular in shape.[9]

1320

Roberti de Greystanes in his *Historia de Statu Ecclesiae Dunelmensis* describes that when the Abbot of the Abbey of Durham died on the feast of St. Gregory, he was buried in the choir of St. Leonard before the great altar.

After his death a great light appeared in the sky and seemed to shine over the burial place. Afterwards the object was seen to descend and move from one place to another.[9]

1290

An old manuscript was discovered in January, 1953, at Ampleforth Abbey describing how in 1290 a flying saucer flew over Byland Abbey in Yorkshire.

The Abbot and the monks were about to commence a meal of roast sheep when one of the brethren ran in to announce a great portent outside. They all ran outside and saw a large round silver disk fly slowly over them.[9]

1254

On the night of January 1, 1254, some monks at St. Albans, England, saw in the sky "a kind of large ship elegantly shaped, and well equipped and of marvelous color."[90]

Sometime during the reign of Charlemagne

A.D. 742-814

During the reign of Charlemagne spacecraft took away some of Earth's inhabitants to show them something of the way of life of space people. These events are described in the Comte de Gabalis's discourses.

However, when the space ships returned bringing back the Earth people they had taken away, the populace were convinced that they were actual members of the spacecraft whom they regarded as sorcerers.

They hurried these innocent people off to be tortured, many of them were put to death.

"One day, among other instances, it chanced at Lyons that three men and a woman were seen descending from these aerial ships. The entire city gathered about them, crying out that they were magicians and were sent by Grimaldus, Duke of Beneventum, Charlemagne's enemy, to destroy the French harvests. In vain the four innocents sought to vindicate themselves by saying that they were their own countryfolk, and had been carried away a short time since by miraculous men who had shown them unheard of marvels, and had desired them to give an account of what they had seen."

The four unfortunates were about to be thrown into the fire by the frenzied populace when they were saved at the last minute by Agobard, Bishop of Lyons. He listened to the accusations and to the defence, afterwards issuing his dictum to the effect that it was untrue the four had fallen from the sky.

The people believed the good Bishop rather than what they had seen with their own eyes and the four 'contactees' (as we would call them today) were set free.[91][92]

Before Christ

218 B.C.

"In Amiterno district in many places were seen the appearance of men in white garments from far away. The orb of the sun grew smaller. At Praeneste glowing lamps from heaven. At Arpi a shield in the sky. The Moon contended with the sun and during the night two moons were seen. Phantom ships appeared in the sky."[93]

This report and many others from Saxon and Roman times have been translated from the writings of the period by W. R. Drake, who is the foremost writer and researcher today in the field of saucers in antiquity. He has delved into the works of Livy, Ovid, Varro, Pliny, Obsequens and many others, providing a rich and valuable treasure house of sightings from those ancient times.

Sometime during the reign of Thutmose III

1504-1450 B.C.

Among the papers of the late Professor Alberto Tulli, former Director of the Egyptian Museum at the Vatican, was found one of the earliest known records of a fleet of flying saucers written on papyrus long, long ago in ancient Egypt. Although it was damaged, having many gaps in the hieroglyphics, Prince Boris de Rachewiltz subsequently translated the papyrus and irrespective of many broken sections he stated that the original was part of the Annals of Thutmose III, *circa* 1504-1450 B.C. The following is an excerpt:

In the year 22, of the 3rd month of winter, sixth hour of the day . . . the scribes of the House of Life found it was a circle of fire that was coming in the sky. . . . It had no head, the breath of its mouth had a foul odor. Its body one rod long and one rod wide. It had no voice. Their hearts became confused through it; then they laid themselves on their bellies. . . . They went to the Pharaoh . . . to report it. His Majesty ordered . . . has been examined . . . as to all which is written in the papyrus rolls of the House of Life. His Majesty was meditating upon what happened. Now after some days had passed, these things became more numerous in the skies than ever. They shone more in the sky than the brightness of the sun, and extended to the limits of the four supports of the heavens. . . . Powerful was the position of the fire circles. The army of the Pharaoh looked on with him in their midst. It was after supper. Thereupon, these fire circles ascended higher in the sky towards the south. Fishes and volatiles fell down from the sky. A marvel never before known since the foundation of their land. And the Pharaoh caused incense to be brought to make peace on the hearth. . . . And what happened was ordered by the Pharaoh to be written in the annals of the House of Life . . . so that it be remembered for ever.[94]

Chinese Taoist writings state that Chen Jen—the 'perfect Man'—was born on the wings of the wind, seated on the clouds of Heaven, and that he traveled from one planet to another.

The Hopi Indians of Arizona and the Navajo Indians, as well as many other tribes, all tell of a time when 'gods' came down from the skies.

The Hindu Vedas and the Bible both cite many examples of space people visiting the Earth. There is the famous biblical account in Ezekiel i, of a spacecraft landing by the river Chebar.

Walter Sullivan, Science Editor of the *New York*

Times, in his remarkable book *We are not Alone,*[95] brings to our attention *The Book of the Secrets of Enoch,* and quotes the distinguished American astronomer, Dr. Carl Sagan, who cited a suggestion from Soviet Russia that Enoch may have been taken on journeys into space.

My native country, Ireland, has more than its share of space visitors. There is the story of Cuchulain who defeated his foes in flying chariots.

All over the world there are the same stories handed down from ancient times of people who came from the skies. Ancient Egypt, India, Japan, China, Scandinavia, Ireland, the Americas, and many other lands, all tell of days when the 'gods' trod this Earth of ours. Since time immemorial we have not been alone.

VIII

WHY ARE flying saucers coming here? This is undeniably a reasonable question, although perhaps somewhat worn from repetition, and apparently not answered to everyone's satisfaction, because "Yes, but . . ." usually follows all explanations as surely as night follows day; nonetheless, for the benefit of newly interested people, we shall explore this once again during the course of this book, and then sit back with a twinkle awaiting the new tidal wave of "Yes, buts . . ."

In the meantime, however, and perhaps of even greater significance, we shall ask an exact opposite question, namely: Why are WE here? This, too, is invariably punctuated by "Yes, buts" instead of question marks; nonetheless, it might be wise if we began exploring this matter without further ado, because right now we consider this planet our very special field of operation as well as our very special home, and I think we'd all agree without a summit conference that it might be very helpful if we happened to light upon the best of all possible reasons for being here—that is, if the simple uncomplicated fact of just 'BEING' isn't good enough.

Dominion, Replenish and *Subdue*—three key words. Perhaps, in a sense, they are magic words, because they seem to hold a certain fascination for us, forming some sort of unwritten law even before we're old enough to understand exactly what they mean or do anything about them.

They come to us in the form of an injunction bidding us have *"Dominion over the Earth," "Replenish the Earth,"* and *"Subdue the Earth."* These messages, then —in the form of a command—tell us much about the nature of our planet right from the outset. They also suggest rather pointedly our reason for being here, and tell us something about the nature of the work we shall be engaged in.

We can justifiably suspect from the use of the word *Subdue,* that our planet is in a raw, or unharnessed, condition requiring a rather large, well-integrated, co-operative adventure to cultivate and tame.

At this point, a chorus of voices may well be heard exclaiming, "Yes, but to what extent or degree should this be done? Hasn't most of it been accomplished already? We have built bridges across nearly all our rivers. We have motor cars nearly everywhere, and planes that can traverse the globe—if they don't run out of fuel in the wrong places. We have manned space capsules orbiting the Earth occasionally and successful satellites constantly relaying a variety of helpful information to us. We also have power plants strewn all over the civilized world furnishing us with electricity. True, we still don't know what electricity is, but we use it anyway!"

All this is unquestionably true, however, the fact remains we find ourselves very much in the same position as Mandy, with the exception that she had no illusions whatsoever about what she was really doing.

The story of Mandy comes to us from the deep South in the United States. She was a faithful family retainer going about the house cleaning business of the day, when her employer called out to her, "Mandy, are you dusting?" "Oh, no sir!" she replied emphatically. "I'm just rearranging the dust!" And wouldn't it seem this is what we may have been doing most ingeniously for a very long time—"rearranging the dust?"

Lately, however, several branches of science have begun probing at and near the source level of life itself. Most notably are those scientists busily engaged in unlocking the secrets of Deoxyribonucleic Acid and Ribonucleic Acid, or DNA and RNA for short. So far these dual acids have proved themselves to be the building blocks *behind all life forms* whether animate or inanimate. Now, it would seem the 'dusting' has begun.

Are these acids DNA and RNA devoid of, or separated in some way from, electromagnetic energy? No, they are not—not really. There's always the power behind the power. Very often this is called quite simply 'a vital force," or 'the vital force.'

Electricity, or electromagnetic energy, falls into this 'vital force' category. Be that as it may, we still don't know what electricity is, but as we said before, we use it anyway! Paradoxically though, we do know what kind of electricity our planet has always generated all by itself without any help from us, and we've named it Direct Current because it flows in one direction only.

We also know that a magnetic field builds up with the current and goes along for the one-direction ride, or maybe it's the strength of the magnetic field that takes the current for the ride, instead. We're not sure which way it is, or which came first, the current or the magnetic field. It's very much like asking, which came first the chicken or the egg? However, we do know that at a given point in its journey the magnetic field reaches its peak and collapses. And the current collapses with it!

Therefore, we must assume that the current is not powerful enough to carry on its journey without the field.

Is that the end of the whole thing right then and there? No, it's just the end of that particular journey. Both current and field fall back to their original starting point and begin the whole trip over again, and over and over again monotonously for ever. We say *for ever*, not because the Earth's currents can't overload and short circuit from purely natural causes, but because even if they do, it'll only be a matter of time until they fix themselves and start the same one-direction collapse ride just as they did before.

Does this sound to you as though the current generated by the Earth beneath our feet has been 'subdued;' or that we have come to have any special 'dominion' over it at source level?

True, because of the genius of one man, Nikola Tesla, we now understand the harnessing principle and have means of taming 'natural' Direct Current as well as the machinery to operate it which Tesla designed and built. It was he who discovered how to keep the magnetic field from collapsing at its peak.

This means is completely ingenious, on the one hand, and yet quite simple in principle. In order to keep the magnetic field and the current from falling backward, one must catch the magnetic field just as it reaches its peak and give it a boost at just the right moment. But, how would one go about doing that, when there's only one circuit and nothing following along behind to give it a boost? Exactly! Create more than one circuit—as many circuits as you wish—and stagger their output, one behind the other, so there's always a booster arriving on schedule just in the nick of time.

So, these many new circuits became known in electrical jargon as *Alternating Current*, the *Multiphase System* (or *Polyphase System*), and the magnetic field, no longer able to boomerang, or collapse, under its own dictates, became known as the *Rotating Magnetic Field*. The one-direction collapsible ride had been turned into Multiple Uninterrupted Journeys Unlimited, and the first step in harnessing natural 'raw' current was accomplished!

Later on in this book you'll hear more about the rotating magnetic field and its connection with the propulsion system used by certain types of flying saucers. Right now, though, let us examine whether or not we think this initial harnessing job should be extended to include the Earth itself. At the present time, all we do is invert it from DC to AC at our power plants atop the Earth's surface, while the Earth continues with its collapsible ride system. In this respect, could it still be said that we are doing nothing more than "rearranging the dust?"

And then, what about man himself? What kind of current is he generating? So far, we know *all life forms* (including planets and suns) generate electromagnetic energy, and that every time man's electrical output has been measured, the amount registered at about 1/10th of a volt, Direct Current. My, what an insignificant amount! But wait. There's always a compensatory law, and this one says: the lower the voltage, the higher the amperage. Now what do you say? Exactly! With a voltage *so-low*, his amperage must have potential to stagger the imagination.

Now, shall we stop a moment to recall our definitions? Amperage and voltage are merely terms of measurement. The amount of current in use is measured as so many amperes, or 'amps,' while the voltage is a measurement term designating how much *pressure* is being applied to the current to make it move. There, it naturally follows that man must be moving a fantastically high current under the minute pressure of 1/10th of a volt, Direct Current!

Does this voltage ever vary from time to time? We

suspect it does; however, so far, no one seems to have caught and measured it while doing so. We also have good reason to suspect that man (the magnificent two-legged animal), along with his four-legged friends, may come equipped with built-in 'inverters' that switch him over to Alternating Current without his knowing it. We also suspect that at least one mammal of the sea, the Bottle-Nosed Dolphin, is similarly equipped. But, we have yet to prove all this; however, there's no question that Mammalia, regardless of species, is truly a remarkable electric generator. And in this we must also include our birds, because although they are not mammals, they are animals and are, therefore, classified correctly as belonging to our kind. If this news is offensive to some ears, it is only because a tremendous confusion has sprung up around the words 'beast' and 'monster.' Actually, there's no scientific connection, or any other, between the latter two words and the word *animal*.

When we stop to consider heat losses incurred by current carried along a single wire, and the rule is: heat losses increase four times when current is doubled, nine times when current is tripled, and sixteen times when current is fourfold, then we see, that what man is doing with his omnipotent current is enough to make one sweat! This is exactly what he does do most proficiently from head to toe. Remarkable? Indeed, he is!

Even so, could we say that his own current has been 'subdued?' Does he have complete 'dominion' over it? Is he, more often than not, subjected to a magnetic field —just as is the Earth—that builds up to its peak and then collapses? In the last analysis it would seem so. Perhaps, then, man was intended to tackle his subduing job at its very deepest point? If that is so, the extent and degree would be very deep, indeed!

IX

FLYING SAUCERS have been observed time and again to have certain repetitive characteristics which are extremely helpful in pointing up intriguing ideas for organized scientific study.

Professor Charles A. Maney, distinguished physicist, and Professor Emeritus of Physics and Mathematics at Defiance College, Defiance, Ohio, has contributed many such intriguing scientific articles on the subject of various UFO characteristics, such as: electro-magnetic effects; Angel Hair; color changes of saucers in flight, and other observable effects.

Perhaps the most astonishing characteristic of all is the ability of the saucers to plummet in and out of our oceans, and other lesser bodies of water, without loss of forward or reverse speed.

Picture, if you will, a 'terminal velocity dive' in *both* directions down and *up!* Incredible! But, there you have it. And all at once 'astonishing' becomes somewhat less than a superlative word.

In an article in *Flying Saucer Review*,[96] Professor Maney listed as many as eighteen examples of electro-magnetic effects by flying saucers.

For example, when in very close proximity, the craft's propulsion mechanisms usually have a notable effect on short wave radio used by our aircraft; gyrocompasses; standard magnetic compasses; magnesyn compasses; cars' ignition systems, as well as their radios and headlights; home radios; television sets; lights and electric meters.

In June, 1960, a study of the same phenomenon by members of the National Investigation Committee of Aerial Phenomena (NICAP), located at Washington, DC, reported there were eighty-one main cases of this nature and nine borderline ones. Then, more recently, another NICAP publication, *The UFO Evidence*,[3] issued a very detailed synthesis of data listing as many as 106 main cases and ten borderline ones. All these were prior to January, 1964.

Professor Maney also cited several examples in his 1958 article in *Flying Saucer Review*.

One instance involved a British airliner bound for Holland on May 31, 1957.[97] It was just passing over Kent when they encountered an oval-shaped UFO. Within seconds the plane's radio became inoperative due to circuit breaker difficulty, but resumed immediate operation the moment the UFO sped away. At no time was the plane's ignition system immobilized.

Then, on the night of November 2, 1957, during the big November 'flap' of that year, a bright egg-shaped object was seen passing low over a highway near Levelland, Texas. The object was reported to be about 200 feet in length, and this time it caused a number of car ignition systems and headlights to fail until the UFO streaked away. As usual, only momentary electrical disruption.

This was a remarkably authenticated case, witnessed by the following law officers:

Sheriff Weir Clem
Constable Lloyd Bollen
Deputy Sheriff Pat McCulloch
Police patrolman A. J. Fowler
Highway patrolman Lee Hargrove
Highway patrolman Floyd Gavin

Another widely publicized incident occurring during the same period on the night of November 6, 1957, near Alamogordo, New Mexico, was that of James Stokes, a research engineer at the US Air Force Missile Development Center, who was driving along Highway 24 when he noticed a 500 foot long elliptical-shaped UFO flying between the area of the Missile Center and White Sands. As the huge object neared the highway both his radio and car ignition system cut out, as did those of *ten other cars* making up the traffic along the highway at that point.[98]

Stokes said that as the UFO passed close to him he felt a tremendous wave of heat. Later upon undergoing a medical examination at Holloman Air Force Base it was discovered he was suffering from sunburn.

In the opposite connection, it is interesting to note that ten years earlier a similar incident occurred in broad daylight involving a very knowledgeable young woman from New York City who was on holiday in Texas. This account has been sent to me by an American correspondent of the highest integrity.

The lady in question was driving along a highway on the outskirts of Fort Worth when a flying saucer about twenty-five feet in diameter glided slowly and silently over the top of her car. Struck by the simplicity and silence of the craft she slammed on her brakes, hopped out and waved ecstatically after it. The saucer pilots noticing the gesture obligingly banked the craft and waved back. Greetings accomplished they flew off about their business and she went on about her own.

It was a metallic disk, she said, bearing no insignia whatsoever, and although she'd never seen or imagined anything like it before, assumed it to be one of her own country's latest aircraft models. Particularly amusing was the fact she lost no time telling her friends about this last word in aircraft development by the USAF. "It's the most beautiful ship you've ever seen and it's *absolutely noiseless!* Isn't that wonderful?"

My correspondent and her friends told her that it was, indeed! But that there wasn't the slightest chance it belonged to the USAF, nor was there much possibility that it even came from this solar system. To this she replied: "I couldn't care less where it comes from. They're for me!"

Unfortunately, this type of sighting is never well authenticated, and this fact in itself is a bit strange. Regardless, it is worthy of note that this model craft *lost no propulsion energy* in heat, did not blister the paint on the lady's car, disrupt the ignition system or give her a sunburn.

Another common characteristic of flying saucers is their extraordinary habit of strewing the countryside with a strange, fibrous substance known as Angel Hair. Once again we are indebted to Professor Maney for his research on this phenomenon.

In an article entitled *The Phenomena of Angel Hair* which appeared in *Flying Saucer Review,* Professor Maney selected from a three-year span, October, 1952, to October, 1955, seventeen incidents of Angel Hair falling from UFOs in different parts of the world. Nor has there been any particular slacking off of this phenomenon since that time.[99]

His list includes the Oloron and Gaillac, France, sightings (covered earlier in this book), as well as falls in New Zealand, Italy, and the United States, specifically Ohio, Illinois, Arizona, California, North Carolina and New York. (You will also recall that earlier Australia's heavy fall of Angel Hair in 1961 was mentioned.)

What *is* Angel Hair? What do we know about it? We know that this stringy fibrous substance has been frequently linked with UFOs, and that it generously drapes itself about the countryside, on telegraph wires, hedges, trees, fields and all over the place. We know that it becomes gelatinous and evaporates shortly after touching the ground, and that when someone picks it up and it touches the skin, the substance disappears!

Today it must be classed as a mystery, because if a chemical analysis has been made of the substance it has not yet been released to the public so far as is known.

There have been many theories put forward about Angel Hair. One saucer researcher, George C. Wilson, connects it with 'manna' from heaven—the same manna that fell in ancient times and was spoken of in the Bible. He also specifically connects it with Mars and believes that a steady fall of edible sugars produced by the sun's rays may form this basic chemical concoction in the Martian atmosphere, and that the ice caps of Mars are not water at all but a carbohydrate we called manna, which distills during the summer on Mars and turns green as it moves towards the Martian equator. He concludes that this is the substance that Martians eat, although why they should drop it all over our planet is not quite clear.[100]

Of course, the main trouble with this theory is that we have much recorded history from all over the world, which has been most ably and carefully compiled by Dr. Immanuel Velikovsky in his book, *Worlds in Collision*,[101] telling us about the characteristics of old-time manna. Probably, the most significant thing was that it didn't disappear when touched, and this is extremely fortunate because it arrived during one of Earth's cataclysmic upheavals when food for survivors was a matter of great urgency; therefore, it was given many different and highly complimentary names, such as 'heavenly ambrosia,' 'bread from heaven,' 'corn from heaven,' and 'bread of the mighty.' It was also continually referred to among Greek authors from Homer to Hesiod as 'ambrosia, the heavenly food which in its fluid state is called nectar,' and was described as having 'the fragrance of a lily,' and 'the taste of honey' combined with an oily flavor. Thus it came to serve as an ointment and as a perfume, besides food—a veritable all-around first-aid kit from heaven.

However, let no one think that all this goodness was dropped off by celestial parcel post from UFOs. Far from it! At that time conditions over the entire Earth and its surrounding atmosphere were so grim that there are grave doubts a single UFO could have got through to deliver a band-aid much less cause rivers to flow with 'milk and honey,' and manage all the rest.

I don't think there's any question that around 13,000 B.C. a natural celestial disturbance of great magnitude caused the Earth's unharnessed electric currents to short circuit. (It must be remembered that we do not yet have 'dominion over' a single planet in this solar system, or any migrant meteor or wandering comet. The entire system is generating raw, unharnessed, Direct Current *au naturel.* Under these circumstances almost anything can happen.)

Oddly enough, the composition of a comet reads almost like a basic master recipe: oil, carbon and hydrogen. One could almost think of it as an orbiting refreshment stand. So, the odds favor eventual proof that it was a comet that passed too close to us which caused one of the worst catastrophes in Earth's history, and served refreshments at the same time.

As to present day Angel Hair, it must be noted that as yet we haven't been able to salvage it much less make Angel Hair cake from it, use it for salad oil, perfume or ointment; so, I don't think we'll have to reciprocate for bonbons from Mars. Nevertheless, we have much to learn about this intriguing substance, and it may be of interest that Mr. Wilson is said to have captured the open-minded attention of the late Dr. Einstein with his ideas, although somehow we suspect they were probably *other* ideas. The fact remains that Angel Hair is a characteristic of flying saucers that frequently recurs and, therefore, must be of considerable scientific interest to proper research of the whole UFO question.

Another characteristic of the saucers is the way they are reported to change color in flight. First, let us tackle the subject of neon (Aurora Borealis) effects of saucers from the standpoint of the visible spectrum, or that portion of the 'octave' sensitive to our visible apparatus.

Colors are nothing more than a series of differing wave-lengths of which the human visual mechanism is only capable (on the average) of perceiving those lying between 3,800 and 8,000 angstrom units. For example 'red' is evoked upon our visual apparatus by waves measuring 760 millimicrons in length (a millimicron is one billionth of a meter!), while 'yellow' is 574.5 millimicrons in length and 'violet' 385 millimicrons.

Very few people can detect color either below red or above violet, although there are techniques even now being developed for lengthening man's visual and color reception. And isn't it about time, too? I am sure you will agree that this is a remarkably short range—a mere 385 to 760 millimicrons! Therefore, in spacecraft we only see color changes our eye mechanisms are equipped to see.

The same holds true of our colorful advertising displayed by neon tubes. We mention the neon tube because the principle of it is the same as the color changes emitted by saucers.

Neon, as you know, is an inert gaseous element found in our atmosphere that when put under electrical pressure in a partial vacuum (tube) emits a reddish glow. This automatically tells you what is happening when you see a flying saucer surrounded by a red glow. (There are many such cases, one of which will be reviewed in the next chapter.) It also indicates, of course, that there is an invisible, partial vacuum-like tube, or screen, around the craft.

Those of you who have a natural bent for physics and mathematics together with the necessary laboratory equipment may now become delightfully absorbed in calculating how much electrical pressure (energy) must be applied to various gases in a partial vacuum in order to produce a riot of colors ranging from red to violet, and what, if any, is the relationship of these colors to speed. It has been generally accepted, you see, that as the speed of the craft increases, so does the luminosity— in effect producing brighter colors.

When the UFO is stationary or hovering it is usually reported to be silvery-gray. Then as it starts to move it turns bright red (accompanied sometimes by a dark patch). As the speed increases it has been said to turn from yellow to white, then green and on to blue, and even purple! But we doubt that this is the correct order. We also think the word 'violet' may have been meant instead of purple. But let us not forget there are different kinds of propulsion systems, so don't be surprised should you happen to see a saucer not emitting any colorful auras at all. They're just easier to spot, of course, when they do.

One of the most fascinating characteristics of flying saucers, as we said before, is their ability to plunge in and out of the oceans at will. There are many records of this phenomenon both prior to and after 1947.

For example, on April 19, 1957, at 11:52 A.M., the bosun and four other crew members of a Japanese fishing boat, *Kitsukawara Maru*, sailing south of Yokohama, spotted two silvery metallic craft descending from the sky. They watched the objects dive into the sea nearby, at about 143' 30" North and 31' 15" East. After the craft submerged there was a violent turbulence. The bosun said the objects had no wings and were nearly disk-shaped. They proceeded to search the area for wreckage but were unable to find anything.[102]

Then, at midnight on Sunday, September 1, 1957, two policemen patroling the sea front at Porthcawl, Glamorgan, Wales, on the Bristol Channel, noticed a glowing bright red object on the horizon with a black zig-zag streak across its center. It was rising out of the Channel![103]

Chief Inspector Reginald Jones, of D Division, Glamorgan Police, stated that at first the two officers thought they'd spotted a ship afire in the direction of Ilfracombe, England. But then the object which was a good deal larger than a full-sized harvest moon and bright red began emerging from the water.

While they watched, two more streaks appeared and took up their stations above and below it. The object remained at sea level for a time and then suddenly took off at a fantastic speed towards the Atlantic.

There have been many reports of UFOs diving into the sea, and often they have been seen to reappear shortly afterward, and fly off at terrific speeds.

Then, in the form of another strange phenomenon, ships sailing the high seas in the areas of the Persian Gulf, China Sea and the Pacific Ocean, have also reported encountering super-constructions in the shape of illuminated wheels.

More than a century ago, according to the *Malta Times*, the crew of the brig *Victoria* sailing just off the Isle of Malta on June 18, 1845, saw three luminous bodies rise out of the sea about a half mile from the ship and watched them for about ten minutes.[83]

Then, Commander Pringle of HMS *Vulture* reported on May 15, 1879, what appeared to be luminous pulsating waves beneath the surface of the ocean. As it drew nearer, passing beneath his ship he could now distinguish what looked like two revolving wheels of light complete with luminous spokes, which amazingly enough took up positions on each side of the *Vulture* and accompanied it for about half an hour.[83]

Very much the same thing happened during May, 1880, on a voyage up the Persian Gulf. Several passengers aboard the *Patna*, a steamer owned by the British India Company, reported being paced on each side of the ship by two enormous illuminated wheels—again, with luminous spokes. There are many more stories about this interesting phenomena and those of you who are intrigued by them will be amply rewarded by looking into the works of Charles Fort.[83]

It seems generally conceded that illuminated wheels and other types of UFOs dive only into the deepest parts of our oceans. This is not quite true as you've probably noticed by the locations of the sightings just related. In fact, spacecraft appear to have such acute control of their craft they could be described as indulging in operations unlimited. They do, of course, plunge into the deepest parts of our oceans, but they've also been seen to plunge into the Pacific just off the beach at Santa Cruz, California, and into the Atlantic of Wallis Sands—a very beautiful beach at Portsmouth, New Hampshire.

Another correspondent of mine in the United States, K. Dorn, of Shirley, Long Island, New York, has sent me the following account of an incident which has some amusing sidelights.

"Aside from a glorious beach, Portsmouth is famous for three things: the Portsmouth Naval Prison and the Submarine Base, and the largest Air Force Base in the world.

"It is common knowledge that a sandy shelf extends outward two or three miles from the beach making a delightful ocean paradise for bathers. Occasionally, a submarine can be seen nosing way out around it to avoid going aground. Jets entertain with practice maneuvers. The SAC ships take off and land. The local-hop airliners groan back and forth on their steady flights from Boston to Portland. Private planes buzz around just for the love of it, and the last touch is a Piper Cub that flies up and down the beach sporting a trailer that advertises the latest bargains in anything from hot dogs to men's wear.

"It was on just such a perfect summer Sunday in 1954 while the beach was crowded with off-duty Air Force personnel that a sight-seeing UFO suddenly arrived upon the scene.

"We wondered afterward how long it may have

waited 'upstairs' trying to find a safe hole through our Sunday air traffic, and finding none decided to do the safe thing—come in by terminal velocity dive.

"Another civilian pilot and myself caught sight of it at somewhere between six and seven thousand feet and mistook it for the fuselage of a DC-6 airliner in serious trouble heading for disaster. (Sometimes when the sun is shining just right on an airplane the wings are invisible.) Aside from horror, our immediate reaction was to run for the coastguard, but then we saw it was coming in on the inside of the sandy shelf so fast and so close to the beach there was no possible way to render assistance then or ever!

"A split second later it was just about eye-level and now with great relief we could see clearly it had no wings or appendages of any sort, and no markings or portholes. It was definitely a UFO!

"As the big splash-down came, I turned slightly to observe reactions on the beach and call out, 'Did you see that?' Many people were looking right at it, but true to the Air Force taking 'off duty' seriously (and who wouldn't?) betrayed no sign other than the shrugging of shoulders and a few raised eyebrows.

"Immediately, I turned back to scan the water just slightly south of impact point as I didn't think the UFO had any intention of putting in at the submarine base to the north. Exactly as calculated, and almost before the spray had settled back on the ocean, the craft shot straight up out of the ocean in a reverse terminal velocity dive, flipped over at a perfect ninety degree angle about 150 feet or so above the water, and flew off without the slightest reduction of speed heading south for Cape Ann, Massachusetts. We'd love to hear the Portsmouth Air Force Base explain that one!"

Parallel to the large increase of space ships in our skies since 1947 there has also been a corresponding number of so-called unidentified submarines seen in various parts of the world. It is known that the Soviet Union has been building submarines, but not all these unidentified submergibles can possibly be pinned on that country, especially not the kind that shoot out of the water and go flying off at incredible speeds in the air! Nor can they be American, because it is well known that only now are Americans in the process of trying to produce a flying submarine.

It is highly apparent from the examples given in these pages that the designing engineers of flying saucers with their advanced technology have long ago produced craft capable of performing with equal efficiency both above and under the water.

One may well wonder why these craft should want to travel under the surface of our oceans. Well, as yet we haven't heard their side of it—not in so many words. However, common sense applied to their mode of operations seems to us to make verbal explanations rather unnecessary and a precious waste of time.

Firstly, let us realize that three-quarters of the Earth's surface is under water. Therefore, the richest scientific knowledge about this planet is there—not to mention the aesthetic value in breath-taking beauty. We ourselves have just discovered the same thing.

Secondly, these advanced technicians are in a position to assess our entire galaxy as a whole and correlate it with other knowledge of the surrounding universe. They know that this 'Sb' classification galaxy which is still unharnessed is half-way through its normal life span, and that the spiral arms are imperceptibly but gradually contracting, while the planets making up our galactial celestial apartment house development are imperceptibly but gradually expanding from the core outward. (Hubble's constant deduces the expansion rate of all planets our size at 0.6 mm. per year.)

Very gradually then, we're acquiring larger land masses, even though we always have two opposing forces at work simultaneously. Even so the gain always seems to be slightly more than the loss. Thus, when we hear the disturbing news, for example, that the Pacific coast of the United States is rising at an alarming rate while the Atlantic coast of the same continent is sinking alarmingly, we know that the actual extent of this normal rise and fall is taking place in imperceptible millimeters requiring millions of years to affect any noticeable change.

We have now presented the picture of the over-all galactial problems shared by us and all other 'Sb' classification galaxies. Now let us look at these problems in more detail.

Since there are no two planets alike anywhere—although each in its raw original state generates Direct Current—one must literally start comparison studies from scratch with only this preliminary knowledge as an aid. Our space visitors, then, are obliged to begin their studies from the tiniest micro-organisms on land and in the sea to the largest life-forms Earth's electrochemistry produces, and this also includes the effects of the Earth's generator on the 'building blocks of life'—deoxyribonucleic acid and ribonucleic acid (DNA and RNA for short). In addition, one must unlock the history of the planet hidden in fossils on land and in the seas, and collect data from layers upon layers of seabed extending ever downward toward the seat of our generator—the Earth's molten core.

These activities fall under the heading of 'field service interplanetary division,' and are not very much different from our own field services except in scope. Our own telephone linesmen, for example, fall in this essential but limited category.

From this, the sensational conjecture has arisen that our space visitors may have already established permanent underwater bases in our oceans and, therefore, an underwater race to match.

Our own pioneering work in underwater research led by Commodore Cousteau, Edwin A. Link and many others, has made us realize that before very long we, too, will have the techniques and facilities to remain submerged for long periods of time. All this, plus imagination, combined with a question that seems to plague a few minds as to whether reality of any sort could possibly lie behind the old legends of mermaids, Neptune and company, has given credence to the aforementioned conjecture regarding our space visitors.

The answer in two letters is No! Temporary bases, yes, because one would try to do as much analytical work as possible on the spot. Aside from observing two fundamental natural laws, the conservation of energy and abhorrence of waste, can you imagine any people so foolish as to commute back to their home planet every five minutes with another handful of ocean bottom? We wouldn't do it! And it won't be long before we'll be setting up underwater laboratories in other people's oceans headed by relay teams, and using the same system in both planetary and space station projects.

In field service there is always a manpower shortage. There's so much to be harnessed, kept in repair and remodeled in any given solar system (each planet is rich in natural resources) that robot service comes in mighty handy—in fact is indispensable. But this is not the same thing as developing a new race for these various projects and duties. It can't be done and win. Or put it another way, it can be done if you prefer to lose. The reason is this: the laws and principles governing creation, sealed off this possibility completely. We can make synthetic substitutes provided they have their root in natural elements, and they do: we can manufacture whole races of robots capable of performing perfectly in our place and construct them out of anything from tin cans to lifelike plastics. We can even program them to reproduce themselves, but we cannot give them a *brand new* personal oscillograph waveform (our individual passports through enternity), not even if we dip into the octaves way beyond our present knowledge.

Originally, all life-forms evolved out of the rich chemistry of the sea, which means out of the ocean or out of deep space. The difference is negligible. A particular niche in the octave predetermined which species to be a 'landlubber,' just as the dolphin, a most lovable and constructive creature known to possess brain development 100 times that of a human on this planet, was destined to be THE mammal of the sea. On our Earth he represents the true underwater race, and is highly qualified to represent us as friendly civilized ambassadors loaded to his flippers with information about a habitat known to him for millions of years.

If we decided to become permanent denizens of the deep we'd be obliged, then, to give up our eternal passports, or niche in the octave, and adopt another suitable to the environment. Not only would this constitute 'regression,' but we'd be usurping the niche of some other entity long in existence and at best come in a poor second, which is a gross understatement when we stop to consider the psychological repercussions.

No, the job everywhere is to bring our real selves— what we are—as well as our natural environment into perfect symmetry and balance. This cannot be done by giving up one's own special waveform. Therefore, no matter how many ocean-bottom laboratories we may establish here or anywhere in the galaxy we'd hardly be so foolish as to become permanent residents in our oceans. The octave that designates us as planetary landlubbers will always hear the call of terra firma, even though we may remember with love and reverence the sea out of which it is said we came and from which all remembrance legends came to be of mermaids and a renowned leader who was finally named Neptune by the Romans and Poseidon by the Greeks. Each stage of evolution has always had its own Winston Churchills, Abraham Lincolns and Mahatma Ghandis.

X

WILLIAM GILBERT, a physician and physicist, who lived in the reign of Queen Elizabeth the First, was the discoverer of magnetism. It was he who first visualized the Earth as a large magnet. In 1600 his great work, *De Magnete*,[104] containing the results of his researches was published.

Three hundred and sixty-odd years have passed since Gilbert wrote his treatise. Today it is known that our planet is an electromagnetic generator, and that all electromagnetic generators produce magnetic force fields even as you and I. We also know that our sun is a very huge master generator busily turning hydrogen to helium for our benefit. Large or small, all generating bodies produce these fields which are carried outward in all directions by imaginary lines called 'magnetic lines of force,' and these lines, in turn, connect with all other generating bodies in the universe, just as all their lines connect with ours. It would seem we have much company although these astronomical number of connections are quite invisible.

Not many years ago our sun and others like it had only two names. With the exception of 'magnet,' it was either called a sun or a star. Today, due to scientific unveiling of its operations, the mysteries have been dispelled and it has acquired two more highly descriptive names in the process. It is known as a magnetohydrodynamics generator (MHD for short), and a hydrogen fusion reactor. All this is by virtue of its ability to combine 'plasma' (ionized gas) of which it is composed, with a magnetic field which converts heat into electrical energy in one step without 'middle-men' mechanical aids and devices. A remarkable feat!

We are now in the process of trying to reproduce this feat in our gigantic laboratories and, of course, running into loads of trouble at every turn. Heat losses are incurred through friction. Our plasma wanders off seeking the great open spaces between magnetic lines of force and has to be 'pinched' back into the crowded throng, or the plasma attracts one too many electrons thereby losing its electrical neutrality which lowers the efficiency and can even short circuit the generators.

Incidentally, all these remarkable generators, just like our sun, only generate raw, natural, Direct Current exclusively. Inverting them to Alternating Current has been considered, but it proved to be impractical as well as uneconomical.

Although, so far as we know, our efforts in this field haven't yet been crowned with wild success, we are confident that eventually the problems will yield to the patient endeavors of man, at which time MHD will be put to many good industrial uses. In addition it may be a good discipline to go back into the field of Direct Current and learn how to reconstruct our sun's activities. What better way to learn how to harness and improve upon them?

The idea of improving such an august body as our sun may sound arrogant in the extreme, yet hasn't it always been the pressing duty of man to refine and improve the raw nature of his planet in order to survive upon it? And as he succeeds in having 'dominion over' his Earth he always sees more that should be attended to which gradually, but naturally, extends outwards to 'source level' projects—*the taming of the raw current beneath his feet* and *the taming of the raw generator above his head*. To bring stability and harmony into his *entire* environment is precisely why man is here.

As you all know, Mariner IV showed us that Mars

has no iron core, no radiation belts, very weak magnetic field, and as a generator is nothing much to write home about; nonetheless, along with Earth and the rest of our planets it is held in its space lane on a predictable course by nothing except laws of magnetic attraction and repulsion—more specifically—by push-pull magnetic forces so evenly distributed and exerted upon every object in the whole universe that they all stay right in their respective flight paths.

Push-pull forces exert the same restrictive influence on all objects upon the Earth, too, whether they be animate or inanimate, otherwise we'd go flying off in all directions along with our can openers, washing machines, and you name it!

The Earth's magnetic lines of force alone measure 1,257 lines per square centimeter in one direction and 1,800 per square centimeter in the other direction, yet, densely as these are packed together not one ever touches the other! This is one of the greatest marvels of nature.

Right here someone is going to say, "What's so marvelous? If they're imaginary I can think them up by the billions and pack them any way I choose." Very true. The only trouble is you won't be able to detect and measure them. Actually, 'imaginary lines' is a term of convenience for very real and unimaginary force fields, enabling one to depict graphically what cannot be seen by the naked eye.

The same marvel is true of our own bodies and all others everywhere. We don't feel these invisible force fields emanating from us, and seldom notice our invisible outside connections unless shifts in magnetic fields on the sun (which are believed to be caused by sun spots) affect our ionosphere causing all sorts of electromagnetic disturbances in the Earth and on it. We notice them particularly with respect to our radio and television receptions. How many times have you tuned in on a channel, or a given number of kilocycles used by a station in your area and were amazed to hear a broadcast originating from a city two or three hundred miles away? It is true that this is more likely to have happened in the United States, nevertheless it has occurred. One moment the 'signal' was clear, the next garbled, and this was probably made even livelier by pistol shots of ear-splitting static. Dependable reception is all but impossible during these times. Or maybe we should say, our invisible connections are all too annoyingly apparent at those times.

Now, we appreciate there are tremendous distances between Earth and say, Mars or Venus. At inferior conjunction the distance from Earth to Venus is 24 million miles, and to Mars over 34 and a half million miles. At their farthest points from us the mileage expands to 250 and 161 million miles respectively. Quite a leap! Even so, we must remember once we leave our atmospheric pressure behind spacecraft move in a thin vacuum where plenty of electromagnetic activity is going on but no resistance as far as space ships are concerned. No force or thrust is required in deep space unless your business is to rendezvous with some object or you're heading for a specific planet in a neighboring solar system.

Flying saucers can travel at virtually unlimited speeds in 'free space,' although we venture to say, because of the unique propulsion system of many of them, they're not hampered as we are by atmospheric deterrents which surround many untold millions of planets. They simply slow down in order not to plough right through them.

The speed of light has been measured at 186,000 miles per second, and even our beginner's experiments with photon engines show that travel at the speed of light is far from a pipe dream. In addition to this good news astronomers recently discovered that 'quasars' (short for quasi-stellar sources)—the astonishing new phenomenon of the heavens that has the world of astronomy agog—have radio waves of such intensity they are a million times greater than those of our entire Milky Way galaxy combined! In this we have energy exceeding the speed of light, thus the theory that nothing can exceed it has been nullified. It may not even be out of the realm of possibility that once we understand the electromagnetic principle behind the emission of these intense radio waves we may be able to adapt them to many useful purposes including spacecraft propulsion which should enable us to flip from one solar system to the next in far less time than British Railways can take us from Ramsgate to London!

Now, in connection with force fields, Orthoteny is a highly intriguing and baffling subject. In 1954, Aimé Michel, a French mathematician and engineer, found that by plotting sightings of spacecraft along a straight line he obtained as many as five during a period of twenty-four hours.[105]

It was thought that this ability to fly in a straight line proved beyond question that flying saucers were intelligently controlled, although models that do not have reason to follow this method certainly show no lack of it. At any rate, in the meantime, Aimé Michel, along with other researchers who adopted his methods in the United States, Spain and other countries, have continued with much success in their research. This straight line research method is known as Orthoteny. Aimé Michel says, "The Greek adjective 'orthotensis' means 'stretched in a straight line.'"

Many of these straight lines have been found to converge at crossover points, and where they do, it has been reported that UFOs execute a 'falling leaf' maneuver and then take off along a fresh alignment.

The interesting thing is these straight lines never seem to shift or change their positions, but instead, remain stable as though they were as embedded as railway tracks. If magnetic field strength is involved in recharging the propulsion systems of spacecraft, isn't it odd these lines do not shift during sun spot periods? How and why many of the flying saucers seem to stick to the same old lines come fair or foul magnetic weather is indeed quite a mystery!

Another oddity that may be connected in some way with Michel's 'straight lines' is called 'old straight tracks,' which are found all over Britain and were in use by salt and tin traders long before the Romans arrived.

These were rediscovered by Alfred Watkins, an amateur archeologist, who wrote a book about them which was published in 1922 called *The Old Straight Track*.[106] Today, in England there is an active group called the Ley Hunters' Club. (A ley is an old English word for straight track.)

In an article published by *Flying Saucer Review*, James Goddard, secretary of the Ley Hunters' Club, gave a lucid exposition of these ancient tracks and how they can be discovered.[107] For those readers who are interested in following up this fascinating subject they may like to know that a quarterly journal, *The Ley Hunter*, is published by the club.

Mr. Goddard explained that a ley is found by aligning as many 'mark points' as possible. These mark points consist of standing stones, stone circles, tumulo (burial mounds), clumps of scotch firs on hilltops (the descendants of earlier clumps) and other artificial landmarks. Once you have found a ley, further marks will turn up as you continue along it.

The fascinating thing is that there is an enormous network of leys all over the country. Sometimes ten of them converge on one point. Where they cross over is usually an important prehistoric landmark, such as Avebury or Stonehenge. It has recently been discovered that at Warminster where there has been much saucer activity since the beginning of 1965, eleven leys have been noted crossing over there. Incidentally, the Ley Hunters' Club are compiling a National Ley Index which will be added to as more are discovered.

It would appear that these leys can also be found in France. A keen ley hunter and saucer researcher, J. A. Dunkin Wedd, on a holiday in Northern France traveled along one of Michel's orthotenic alignments with some surprising results. He found a clump of *silvestris* at Meursanges and more of them at Le Tertre. These seemed to mark cross-over points for saucers. Scots pine, too, is often linked closely with mark points of leys, as Alfred Watkins has pointed out.

Of course, the field is wide open begging for more research on the connection between Alfred Watkins' 'straight tracks' and Michel's 'straight lines.' There would seem to be one, but this must be corroborated and correlated before we'll be absolutely sure. As you see, it's a highly interesting field justifiably in need of attention.

We can't help wondering, too, whose the first leymen were. Who were the builders of this mammoth network of straight lines and markers? Do these leys exist in other countries than England and possibly France? Were they constructed by some ancient highly advanced civilization on Earth in co-operation with space people at a time many eons ago when open contact between our worlds seems to have existed? And later, is it possible these old tracks and markers were maintained by tin and salt traders plying their wares along these routes? Perhaps so.

These and many more intriguing facets await follow-up research. The Ley Hunters' Club is doing a remarkably good job of work but they need many more members to enable them to carry out their vast program. Who's for ley hunting?

In addition to leys, here and there all over the world

there are quizzical markings in the Earth's surface which can only be seen to best advantage from the sky.

In England, for example, there is the celebrated Uffington White Horse lying under the crest of White Horse Hill on Berkshire Downs. The age of this enormous figure is uncertain, except that it is the oldest of any of the white horses carved on English soil.

True, this figure can be made out from ground level due to its prominent position above White Horse Vale and on a clear day observed from a distance of fifteen to twenty miles; however, inasmuch as it is 365 feet in length, it can only be seen in its true perspective from the air, so we must assume it was meant to be seen that way! Most certainly it becomes an outstanding landmark, showing off its true proportions from a very long way off, when viewed from an airplane.

Another landmark of gigantic proportions is situated in the Glastonbury, Somerset, area in the West of England—an amazing example of prehistoric earthworks. It has been called the Temple of the Stars and occupies an area ten miles in diameter—an enormous planetarium whose hills and artificial waterways depict the signs of the zodiac, reproducing a grand scale map of the heavens that only ages of geological upheaval could possibly destroy, and it bears within the elements of its design surprising evidence that it is older than the Great Pyramid.[2]

Full credit for the discovery in our times of this most ancient testimonial to Man must go entirely to the late Mrs. K. E. Maltwood, who first traced the figures on the ground and arranged to have them photographed from the air. It is from this aerial view, of course, that this Temple of the Stars stands out so convincingly in bold relief. A casual walker on the ground, unless he knew what he was looking for, would not notice anything out of the ordinary. It was meant to be seen from the air.

Then, in Peru, South America, the famous Nazca

Lines were discovered not many years ago by two Peruvian pilots flying at 4,000 feet between Nazca and Palpa, Peru.

Beneath them on the sandy desert, they began to make out figures of birds and other designs—one of a man wearing a crown—and, in addition, discovered literally hundreds of radiating straight lines.

Unless, thousands of years before, the Incas had arrived by air, which is highly improbable, this extraordinary network of radiating lines seems to have been missed by them completely. The fact that they constructed their great coastal road straight through the pattern of lines tends, more than anything else, to indicate this is so. Later, the Incas were plundered by the Spanish. Other peoples came and left passing over the same area heaven knows how many times, yet apparently no one saw them. It remained for two modern airmen to discover them from the air.

Curiously enough, these lines and figures cannot be spotted from a low 'hedgehopping' altitude. The full design only reveals itself from high in the air.

A German scientist, Maria Reiche, has made a deep study of the Nazca Lines and states that the unusual climatic conditions must have had a remarkable preservitive effect because in all probability they are thousands of years old. She has also come to the conclusion that the figures of birds and other designs were made at a much later date than the lines.

George Hunt Williamson, in his book, Road in the Sky,[108] give as detailed account of the Nazca Lines which includes fascinating conversations he held with Maria Reiche and Peruvian Air Force officers about them.

Is it possible these straight lines viewed from high altitudes above Nazca mark strong magnetic force fields? If not, are there places in the world that do mark magnetic power centers where the saucers can refuel?

It is remarkable how many high mountains like Mount Kilimanjaro in East Africa, Mount Rainier and Mount Shasta in the United States, have been reported as places where UFOs have been seen to hover for long periods of time.

Why do so many straight tracks converge on Stonehenge? Could this be another power center? And why were the famous blue stones brought all the way to Stonehenge from the Prescelly Hills in Wales? Did the blue stones have some special properties? Did they act, perhaps, as a kind of condenser for building up electromagnetic power in the same way that piezoelectricity does in twenty different classes of crystal structures?

Now, the subject of the piezoelectric effect in quartz crystals, such as barium titanate, lead zirconate-titanate, and many others, is long, complicated and fascinating—far too complex to do it justice in a few short paragraphs. Suffice it to say, because of the atomic structure they can store energy, step up transformers, and produce voltages up to 20,000 volts without straining at it.

For example, a three-quarter inch long lead zirconate titanate cylinder only three-eighths of an inch in diameter can produce up to 35,000 volts with an applied force of 10,000 pounds per square inch! Per small volume of material their storage capacity is in excess of twenty-five joules per cubic centimeter—truly fantastic, and not at all out of the realm of possibility that certain of the saucers' electromagnetic propulsion systems are able to utilize the piezoelectric effect. In this case shall we say as a booster?

Alan E. Crawford, an authority on the subject of this effect in crystals, wrote a fascinating article on piezoelectricity which appeared in *Discovery* magazine.[109] For those of you who are interested in studying further this much overlooked phenomenon, several books on

113

piezoelectricity are listed in the Bibliography at the end of this book.[110] [111] [112]

In an earlier chapter we discussed Direct Current and how Tesla discovered how to keep the magnetic field from collapsing at its peak through his 'multiphase' or 'polyphase' system, which came to be known as Alternating Current. The one-direction collapsible ride had been turned, you'll remember, into Multiple Uninterrupted Journeys Unlimited.

This all brings to mind a remarkable spacecraft sighting, and once more we are deeply indebted to Professor Maney's research into it, and subsequent experiments of an ingenious and brilliant nature performed by Alan Watts.[113]

Mr. Wildman was delivering a new estate Vauxhall car to Swansea, Wales, during the early morning hours of February 9, 1962. He was just at the end of the deserted Ivinghoe road at Aston Clinton when he noticed an object ahead of him that was white and oval-shaped, with evenly spaced black markings around it which may have been portholes or air vents. The object was twenty or thirty feet above the road and at least forty feet wide.[114]

As Mr. Wildman's car came within sixty feet of it the power of the car's engine dropped down to twenty miles an hour. He changed to second gear, pressed the accelerator flat to the floor without any results whatsoever. The curious thing is, that although his engine lost revolutions his headlights remained bright—never faded at all. Then, the object which, by the way, was quite silent, permitted him to come within twenty feet of it for a distance of some 200 yards before coming down even lower. And so they traveled along this way till they came to the end of the stretch, at which point a white haze like the Moon's halo appeared around the craft and it took off to the right at terrific speed and vanished. Frost particles from tree tops were flecked back upon his windshield as it did so. Although the object was quite solid, because it reflected back his headlights, Mr. Wildman reported no excessive heat from it, nor was the paint on the new car damaged in any way.

Before we continue with what was learned from this sighting, please remember that the ignition systems of cars generate Direct Current.

Thomas Thomson suggested in the British *Luforo Bulletin*[115] that the power loss was perhaps due to the craft's magnetic field affecting the ignition system of the car.

Then Alan Watts hit upon the brilliant idea of winding around a cardboard former a coil of enameled copper wire—616 turns—which he placed over the ignition coil of another car—a Victor. With the engine idling Watts sent a direct current through the fabricated coil. Nothing happened. Then he tried alternating current from eight to 11.5 amperes at fifty cycles per second. Bingo! There was a marked falling off of engine power. He immediately calculated with a physic formula that an alternating magnetic field of the order of 500 units (oersteds) had produced this effect. Noting that the approximate distance from the UFO to the car was twenty feet, he also calculated by the inverse square law that the magnetic field strength one foot outside the saucer was in this case, 200,000 units (oersteds). A very strong magnetic field. He also commented: "Such field strengths can be approached in the laboratory today using super-conducting magnets."

It is also interesting and important to note that the magnetic field strength at a distance of sixty feet from the UFO was nine times greater than at twenty feet— one million eight hundred thousand units (oersteds)!

Still another sighting discussed by the noted scientist Wells Alan Webb bore a striking similarity in association with a super-powerful alternating magnetic field, although in this one, which Mr. Webb has recorded in his new book *Mars the New Frontier*,[116] there are two notable differences, one of which is very important. The craft's propulsion system utilized the Faraday Effect, an entirely different principle based on the relation of polarized light in a powerful magnetic field. The second one difference which we think is of secondary importance, the craft was not oval-shaped but cigar-shaped.

The question we may well ask at this point is why do these superpowerful alternating magnetic fields only slow direct current ignitions down or stop them temporarily with only momentary inconvenience? Why don't the ignition systems short circuit just as does an AC electric appliance when it's plugged into a DC outlet?

We put this question to an electrical engineer who replied promptly: "Alternating Current and Direct Current are both compatible and incompatible at the same time. In this case (referring to Mr. Wildman's sighting) the ignition system did not short circuit because the current was only neutralized like this." Then he drew the following diagram to show how the nodal points from two types of currents meet.

We shouldn't wonder if this isn't the same reason why airplane and car radios are only temporarily hushed until the UFOs speed away again.

PART TWO

POINT OF ORIGIN

All the same, there is no reason to suppose that galactic communities around other star systems have not accomplished interstellar flight long ago.

JAMES STRONG
(Extract from his book *Flight to the Stars*.)

XI

WHERE DO the saucers originate? This bewhiskered question is in need of a good tonsorial job by a Delilah. A Delilah, by the way, is an outmoded word for Personna!

There are many theories, of course, or let us say there *were* many theories putting forth the Moon, Mars, Venus and other planets of our solar system as possible points of origin. However, by the time this goes to press our information, together with what we've already learned from the Venus probe, Ranger VIII (Moon) and Mariner IV (Mars), will show conclusively our space visitors do not originate from this system.

It has also been suggested that bases may have been established on our planets to serve as stop-over points and observation ports. Certainly our visitors could understand Earth better by surveying our surrounding environment, and have undoubtedly sent in technicians

117

for the purpose, but we must point out how much more efficient and comfortable the use of spaceliners are for stop-overs and observation posts. We would suggest that the latter have been used almost exclusively.

Even the famed scientist, Dr. Hermann Oberth, who will be remembered for his pioneer work on the V-1 and V-2 rockets and his constant, invaluable help as a consultant, does not believe our visitors come from this system.

After dismissing the idea that saucers were secret devices of either the Americans or the Russians, he suggested in his article published by *Flying Saucer Review* that they came from the sky (Greek, 'uranos'—hence the Uraniden hypothesis), and since it was not likely our form of life was capable of evolving on other planets in this solar system it was far more probable our elusive visitors came from outside it.[117]

Then, there was an early US Air Force report suggesting that saucers came from the star system Wolf 359.[12] Now, there's an entertaining thought! Could it be because Wolf 359 maintains a steady heat without tendency to fall in scale? Could be. However, it's a blue-white star 'hot as blue blazes' with a temperature over 18,000 degrees Centigrade—three times hotter than our yellow 'G2' classification sun, which means that to produce our form of life any planet circling it would have to be at least three times farther away than Earth is from its little G2 generator. Incidentally, Wolf 359 and other 'Wolf stars' were named after a renowned scientist bearing that surname.

Still another theory has been advanced recently by scientists. They say it is quite conceivable that there may exist a kind of looking-glass universe in which all matter is made up of anti-matter. Could it possibly be that some of the saucers emanate from this reverse side of our energy scale?

This speculation launches us into a highly complex

118

subject requiring a book unto itself. However, as a guide may we point out that we only utilize *one* of sixty-three known octaves (wave-lengths). Beyond them and between them are octaves unlimited which are just as invisible to us as the backside of our one little scale. It is wise to keep this in mind while mentally exploring the looking-glass proposition. We also think the word 'anti-matter' may not have been the best of all possible choices to describe what could be likened to an invisible Xerox copy of our universe.

You are probably saying at this point, well, if this looking-glass universe really exists maybe we're the copy instead. Quite true, we could be, yet it wouldn't make any appreciable difference one way or the other. Without our universe there'd never be any forthcoming proof that the other existed at all, and vice versa. So, in any case, both would be inseparable and completely dependent upon one another.

And lastly, a theory that purports to have been advanced seriously by a few writers on the flying saucer subject is the claim that saucers may come from the interior of our Earth! Needless to say, every unexplained knot-hole on the Earth's surface from the poles to the equator has been given a 'piece of the action.'

Seriously though, it's interesting how those not mentally equipped to deal with abstracts and are not on speaking terms with their unconscious, or alternate brain lobes, always have a psychological need to invent something 'real' that exists in an 'interior.' The fact that we already know the conditions making up the interior of our Earth makes no difference.

Once again. In unison, if you please! The core is a molten generator, the seat of powerful, shifting magnetic fields extending nearly to the Earth's surface. They are unharnessed and to a large degree unpredictable and subject to every sun spot whim our sun is heir to. Sometimes it's all but impossible to stay alive on the surface, the earth beneath is so turbulent. Obviously then, a race of highly advanced technologists would be obliged to stabilize both topside and core before venturing downward to set up permanent housekeeping. So that's that! And we haven't even mentioned what our underground nuclear testing has done to the interior. However, with this thought it is best to fortify oneself with a large economy-size bottle of aspirin!

Now, we take up the subject of what has been observed so far by plain ordinary telescopes from four to sixty-inch lenses. You can have a field day of fun with a telescope. You can even have a picnic with an ordinary pair of opera glasses! Given time and the right conditions you'll eventually see haloes, squares, crosses, walls, lights, triangles, bridges, bumps and ridges—absolutely everything from soup to nuts! This is because the 'boiling' of our heavy atmosphere makes light-rays wobble and this wobbling in turn distorts the celestial images producing the effect of gazing through a defective window pane. In addition, many light rays never pierce our atmosphere at all. They are deflected and sent off on errands elsewhere. Others are absorbed by dust particles and converted to heat. Oh, you can have a jolly time with a telescope!

It is because of these difficulties plus our position in the galaxy—we're located only one-third of the way out from the crowded center, likened to a third floor tenement view—that, for the sake of accuracy, we've come to depend on radio telescopes backed up by cameras and spectroscopic analysis. Works very well, too, considering the handicaps.

Anyway, without these aids what has been seen is rather rich.

Starting with J. Madler, a famous and conservative selenographer who published a map of the Moon back in 1837, we have a square on the edge of Mare Frigoris which he calculated to be sixty-five miles in length and was punctuated by a perfect white cross in the center. The square was backed up by another famous selenographer, E. Neison, who described it as "about sixty-five miles in length, one mile in breadth, and from 250 to 350 feet high," but apparently he didn't see a cross. Neither did the Rev. T. W. Webb; now that's odd because in his book *Celestial Objects* he only added the observation that the walls were "a mile or more thick." Today, our telescope astronomers must feel shot with luck when they only see three sides of the square. One of the sides has disappeared!

Then in July, 1953, the late John J. O'Neill, former science editor of the *New York Herald Tribune*, observed through a four-inch telescope with a magnifying power of 250 what he described as a gigantic natural arch spanning twelve miles from pediment to pediment. A month later, the noted British astronomer, the late Dr. H. P. Wilkins, using a sixty-inch reflector telescope at Mt. Wilson Observatory, saw the arch over Mare Crisium but pointed out that it was only two miles wide. The difference was due to the size of the telescopes. He also explained that because O'Neill's instrument was far less powerful what he'd mistaken for sunlight streaming beneath the arch was nothing more than shadows cast by two promontories.[8]

Dr. Wilkins believed this bridge to be a natural phenomenon, while Willy Ley, for instance, considers it an optical illusion. And despite the fact Dr. Wilkins sighted one UFO over Mt. Etna and three more during a daytime airline flight in the USA, he probably felt they came from other distant parts of our galaxy, although he did not rule out finding life-forms of some sort on Mars and Venus. Further, after many years study, he concluded the Moon was quite sterile, and Ranger VIII proved him to be quite correct!

Considering all the information relayed back to us from the Moon it is not at all surprising that a reddish outline around the Alfonso crater was observed at the Crimea Observatory on November 3, 1958, by the Soviet scientist, Nikolai Kozyrev, who obtained twenty photographs of the volcanic eruption. Dr. Wilkins also spotted a volcano on the Moon and this was reported in the London *Daily Telegraph* of November 21 that year.[118]

The following April, 1959, Dr. Harold C. Urey, Nobel Prize winner and authority on the chemistry of the stars, reported that the Moon which for so long had been thought of as a dead satellite might actually turn out to be a very active body with a hot interior and an erupting shifting surface. And as we all know the compilation of data and pictures sent back recently by Ranger VIII proved Dr. Urey absolutely right.

Not only does the Moon possess a molten core like Earth's with shifting magnetic fields, but its surface is even more unpredictable than ours due to attracting all the celestial garbage in its neighborhood. Aside from the protection afforded Earth by courtesy of the Van Allen belts, the Moon helps out in a sort of minesweeper capacity, accepting a constant meteor pelting full in the face while receiving no comfort from its turbulent interior. The poor old man in the moon really gets it in spades seven ways from Sunday!

This is what accounts for the sudden appearance and disappearance of white domes, black bands and craters, for ever changing their shape. As to the latter, Dr. Wilkins drew our attention to two small ones located in the Sea of Fertility called Messier and Pickering, which become larger then smaller shifting from oval shape to triangular with utter abandon.

As if that wasn't enough for one small satellite measuring only 2,160 miles in diameter, it must also contend with solar winds (strong electromagnetic currents from the sun) that play across the Moon's very thin atmosphere causing it to light up first in one place and then another. Again we have the Aurora Borealis effects, and for the same reason! This explains why the volcanic mountain peaks suddenly become illuminated, then dim, then brighten again and so on, depending on the amount of pressure packed by the solar winds.

XII

MARS IS CALLED the Red Planet because two-thirds of it has always appeared rosy-orange in color. The reasons for the color have been speculated upon time and again. Aside from the oxidation of surface iron theory advanced decades ago, we know for a fact that blue rays have a tendency to scatter profusely and are attracted to and absorbed by Earth's atmosphere (why our sky appears blue, incidentally), thus causing planets and other stars in our galaxy to appear a little more red than they actually are simply on the basis that the blue rays have been absorbed down here.

We didn't have another reason, or at least none came to mind, until after the data and pictures from Mariner IV were received. We learned the atmospheric density is only one to two per cent that of Earth's with only a trace of water vapor, and that the main gases found were carbon dioxide, nitrogen and eight per cent argon. There are other gases in smaller percentages and we suspect one of these may be our old friend neon.

We also discovered that Mars' surface was almost exactly like the Moon's, except that it has no molten core and no turbulent shifting magnetic fields with which to contend. Indeed, its magnetic field strength is very weak; yet, it has been receiving celestial garbage full in the face for millions of years. Like the Moon it has no protection from this. It, too, is beaten by solar winds, and we suggest the pressure of these electromagnetic currents through what little neon and other gases there may be (aside from the three main ones) help the rosy-orange color along.

Since 1877 when Giovanni Schiaparelli discovered lines on the Martian surface which he named 'canali,' there have been quite a few scientists and amateur astronomers who have earnestly believed there were canals on Mars—canals of either natural original, or super-constructed by highly intelligent beings for irrigation purposes. A few even went so far as to imagine a highly melodramatic situation in which these beings were desperately trying to survive upon a planet drying up beneath their feet.

One of these was the famed Professor Percival Lowell after whom the observatory at Flagstaff, Arizona, is' named. He even concluded that certain dark spots where the lines crossed might possibly be Martian cities.

Today, it would seem the French astronomer, Eugene Antoniadi, was probably right when he suggested in 1929 that the 'canali' were simply optical illusions created by difficulties trying to see over immense distances through our very dense atmosphere. Nonetheless, others postulate that all Martian urban activity really takes place beneath the surface, and there is even a theory abroad that the outer layer photographed by Mariner IV is in reality a canopy erected many miles above the actual surface of the planet—suggesting a race of technologists capable of artificial lighting on a global basis, the manufacture of oxygen, and so on and on into infinity.

If it weren't for the stumper involving the percentage of gases making up Mars' thin atmosphere, plus the astonishing scarcity of water vapor, one could actually envision a race of people holing up beneath the surface of a planet where no molten core creates tremendous force fields for ever on the move and for ever on the verge of making themselves unpleasantly known beneath one's feet. But alas! Even those visiting this system from other parts of our galaxy would find it more expedient, I should think, to commute or camp out in huge spaceliners than fool around with such a primitive place as Mars. The extent of work required there simply staggers the imagination, and why begin such a mammoth project until we're at least in a position to lend a few billion helping hands—not to mention a few billion helping heads.

At the moment the usefulness of Mars isn't screaming at us in bold headlines, but with imagination and scientific skills we'll undoubtedly come to recognize its value in extra resources, and end up growing some helpful organism on it, if Mars hasn't already been doing a big business in that department for millions of years.

Currently, the most intriguing puzzle concerns the peculiar behavior of Phobos, one of the two tiny satellites orbiting Mars which were discovered way back in 1877 by the American astronomer Asaph Hall. These are the only two satellites in our solar system, with the exception of those artificially launched from Earth, that revolve around their parent planet in circular equatorial orbits, yet radio telescopic and spectroscopic analyses have shown both Phobos and Deimos to be only ten and five miles in diameter respectively, and composed of volcanic rock.

Deimos is orbiting Mars at a respectful distance of 14,600 miles, while Phobos takes the route of familiarity at 5,800 miles. And route of familiarity it truly is, because Phobos is falling inward (which is known as tidal retardation) while Deimos which should be following suit is spectacularly not doing so. Secondly, Phobos' tidal retardation is much too fast! Of course, it won't crash on Mars for another twenty million years or so, but that's beside the point. Phobos is not artificial, and yet it's behaving as though it was. Now, correlating all the data released by Mariner IV, can anyone deduce from it exactly what ails Phobos?

This seems to be the only phenomenon that eluded the prescience of the noted and beloved Jonathan Swift, who, as you'll remember in his *Gulliver's Travels*,[119] written *150 years* before Asaph Hall discovered the satellites, described both Phobos and Deimos with uncanny accuracy—their distances from the planet, their respective sizes, their strange orbits and many other details which preclude any mathematical probability of pure coincidence.

Although remembering Jonathan Swift at this juncture is somewhat of an aside, the calibre of prescience he represents is truly fantastic, isn't it?

By what electromagnetic-chemical process does this ability operate? There is an answer, of course, even to this baffling question and who knows, perhaps one of our readers is destined to find it.

XIII

VENUS, by far the loveliest sight in the morning or evening sky, is the planet closest to our Earth in both distance and size, although it is considerably younger than our home in space according to Dr. Immanuel Velikovsky, who will doubtless be proved quite correct about it before very long.

Perpetually shrouded in a mantle of clouds, Venus hides all her charms from our prying eyes. She represents a planet of true mystery, conjuring up many baffling questions for us.

Statistically, the planet is second in orbit from the sun. Mercury has the front row seat, and as you know, Earth is in third place.

Two more interesting statistics are comprised in the information that Venus is famous for its 'ashen light' that shines weakly on the night-side of the planet! Recently, however, this has been most interestingly and, perhaps, accurately explained by a notable physicist, John Campbell, in his editorial in the September 1965, issue of *Analog* magazine.

The other interesting statistic is that a recent and successful American probe received back information by telemeter process that the surface of Venus is 800 degrees Centigrade! Anything but that had been anticipated by all so far as we know, except one man, Dr. Velikovsky.

As far back as 1950, and contained in the last chapter of his *Worlds in Collision*,[101] Dr. Velikovsky stated that the surface temperature of Venus must be very hot due to its violent birth. And among other brushes there were "two encounters with the Earth accompanied by discharge of potentials between these two bodies caused by conversion of momentum into heat."

Other astronomers of note had placed the temperature at minus 25 degrees Centigrade; plus 14.2 degrees Centigrade; plus 17.5 degrees Centigrade and on up to plus 30 degrees Centigrade. Not until 1961 was it discovered with no little surprise that the temperature was almost 600 degrees—the last thing ever expected of Venus. Today, on-the-scene telemetering service gives us the more highly accurate figure of 800 degrees. We can believe it!

•   •   •

However, it is possible we have been a little dogmatic in advancing the view that there is no intelligent life in this solar system. The information telemetered back by our satellites indicates this viewpoint to be correct, but we cannot be absolutely certain until we have actually landed on the planets ourselves. There may, too, be intelligent life on the planets capable of evolving in environments where human life could not survive.

Although we know very little about conditions on those planets comparatively close to Earth, our knowledge about the farthermost planets in this system is pretty well nil. At the time of writing no information has been telemetered back from Jupiter, Saturn, Uranus, Neptune and Pluto. Therefore, although the satellite information received so far tends to confirm the scientific view that there is no intelligent life in this system, it is important to keep the mind open on the point of origin of the flying saucers.

XIV

IF WE ACCEPT the evidence that our visitors have been watching us for a very long time (and how could we possibly reject it?) then immediately something hits us in the pineal gland (modern translation of 'between the eyes!') Their technology must be truly fantastic!

We have heard tales of spaceliners several miles in length hovering high above the Earth. Maybe, some of us have smiled politely and dismissed the idea as sheer nonsense. Yet, aside from the fact they've been observed by our own competent pilots, we must remind ourselves that even our small jet airliners have almost reached obsolescence and are now being replaced by larger and larger ones. The new Concord supersonic job, for example, will be something of a leviathan.

In time, our own spaceliners will definitely be enormous flying cities, possibly several miles in length. They will have to be for economic reasons—we shall have to follow laws of conservation of energy and minimize waste. The manpower and robot power we'll be obliged to transport to the 'backward' planets of our solar system will have to be almost astronomical in numbers in order to harness and put them into operation for constructive use. Robots will be used for Venus and Mercury, as well as some of the other planets.

First, we must learn to overcome gravity and inertia

as our space visitors have done, and then we'll be on our way. Nothing is impossible with God. Even the many scientific-natural-spiritual laws (these cannot be separated) which we do not as yet understand fully will become second nature to us almost before the ink is dried, and much that seems beyond us at present will all be accomplished.

Technology alone is not enough. Throughout the entire world every facet of our lives must be streamlined and synchronized to meet the personal and public demands of the new age. Any country in the world today that thirsts for power in the old 'dark age' political sense, or that insists upon hiding behind 'iron curtains' is not only wet behind the ears but will wind up thoroughly drenched when it misses the boat altogether.

Nor can we go on being strangled in legal red tape, and buried daily under tons of paper in triplicate. The people are kept so busy buying glasses to read the fine print, and trying to find someone who can wade through and translate into plain English voluminous tax papers, they haven't found out yet this is the Space Age. They think it's the Paper Age!

However, we have already made tremendous strides. We are on the threshold of becoming full-fledged members of our galaxy, provided we do not listen to factions that would defeat man's purpose simply for the sheer malevolent joy of doing so, and provided we do not turn new-found sources of energy back upon ourselves or invade the provinces of others with them. We must learn to understand what the sado-masochistic drive is, how it operates, find its physical electromagnetic cause, and how to harness and tame it within ourselves, which is what past civilizations—now long forgotten and extinct—failed to do.

A mad all-out effort to catch up with the technology of our space visitors is fruitless. They began eons ago, and are even now still advancing rapidly. Our job is to learn indirectly from them by watching their craft at every opportunity and thinking it out on our own as much as possible.

One reason for their seeming elusiveness is that our planet and natural laws governing it are not identical with theirs. To make exact copies of their craft would be foolish. The general thread of consistency runs throughout the galaxy, but in detail we'll invent modifications more suitable to our individual needs. It is of primary importance that we take special care to preserve the individuality of each habitable planet throughout the galaxy. This is something our space visitors appreciate full well. They, too, know the old saying, "Monkey see, monkey do." Up to a point it's fine, but on a galactial and intergalactial basis it won't hold perfectly.

Do you begin to understand why our visitors are prone to be elusive? Why they pretend they don't want to be seen? They also know that Earthlings adore puzzles, and enjoy figuring them out, and if they make it a point to stay just out of reach but in sight a good deal of the time, you can bet we'll scramble to copy them and ingeniously invent what we can't copy.

XV

A REMARKABLE talk on the BBC Third Program was recently given by I. J. Good, a Fellow of Trinity College, Oxford. Mr. Good works at the Atlas Computer Laboratory of the Science Research Council. A full report of his talk was published in *The Listener*.[120]

Mr. Good spoke about possible life outside the Earth and speculated to some extent on the theme that there may have been millions of advanced civilizations in the galaxy. Some of these might be extinct but by now there might be one great civilization which would have been able to colonize the whole galaxy.

On first thought, one would tend to agree completely with Mr. Good's logic. Such a thing could conceivably occur. At the same time one is reminded of Charles Kettering's hilarious remark that: "Logic is an organized way of going wrong with confidence."

One of the basic laws of Creation ensures that life will automatically evolve out of the electrochemistry of one's own individual stamping grounds, requiring no aids in this department whatsoever (assuming, of course, that a given planet is so situated from its sun that our form of life naturally results).

In our case, what we have already learned from the DNA and RNA factors—the building blocks of life—prove beyond any doubt we evolved out of our own oceans with an aid only from our hydrogen fusion reactor 'upstairs'—the sun. So, also, did Mr. Good's 'great civilization' evolve out of theirs (which I have no doubt exists), and so did all other civilizations in a universe bursting its seams with Sb classification galaxies.

After this was long since accomplished, there seems little doubt a space neighbor of ours from a system that also produces our form of life (and perhaps there are several of these) dropped by to pay us a social call, and stayed like Sheridan Whiteside, in the play *The Man Who Came to Dinner.*

Heaven knows their technology was far in advance of ours and there was plenty of work to do here. We needed helping hands—a neighborly assistance.

The Hopi and Navajo Indians of North America; the Maya and the Inca's people of South America; the Aborigines of Australia; the Hawaiians and the Irish, all have legends and folk-lore telling of a time long ago when the 'gods' came down from the skies. The Hindu Vedas, the Brahman Tablets, as well as Greek, Scandinavian, Tibetan and Japanese tradition all tell the same story of an age when the 'gods' walked the Earth.

The Bible states it quite plainly, too.

> And it came to pass, when men began to multiply on the face of the Earth, and daughters were born unto them. That the sons of God saw the daughters of men that were fair. And they took them wives of all which they chose.
>
> Genesis vi. 1-2

The fact remains that the alliance didn't work out too well, although no great harm was done either.

(1) Regardless how brilliant our neighbors compared to us, they were unable to deduce the basic physical reasons for our tardy development.

(2) The density of Earth's atmosphere produces a strange, one could even say, blinding hypnotic effect, that over a period of time dulls the vision, overpowers clarity of judgement, and in effect drags one into a seemingly hopeless vicious circle, from whence, no doubt, we get the saying, "Misery loves company."

These space neighbors didn't need our women for wives. They undoubtedly had wives at home, and it was no great problem to go back to their planet and fetch them here.

(3) Perhaps they had the notion that their genetic carry-over from offspring by mixed marriages would predominate. Alas! History has shown it did not. We know now that the density here is such that predominating characteristics will inevitably fall back to their original source—our own oceans and our own sun. This time we'll stay alert and insist upon first things first. And in this respect we can help our space neighbors by reminding them how foolish it would be to be sucked once again into our vortex when all we need is a remodeling job from source level outward. After that we

are free and clear to intermarry throughout the galaxy as our hearts dictate.

As to the evidence that they came to Earth and lived here long ago, we have huge monoliths, rock drawings and other artifacts that have survived the ages, proving that a mighty sun-worshipping civilization existed and covered the greater part of the Earth's surface.

This great race was capable of erecting massive buildings containing 200-ton stones and nothing like their work has been equalled by our modern civilization. Today, with all our mechanical wonders it is very doubtful if we could erect such perfect examples of the art of masonry.

We do know that a great catastrophe overwhelmed the world about 15,000 years ago. All that has survived of that prediluvian civilization are a few remnants of that wonderful masonry scattered here and there across the planet. Today, they are a reminder and seeming anathema to some few scientists who cannot accept that any civilization, possibly more advanced than their own, could have existed on Earth more than 8,000 years ago.

The so-called Fortress of Sacsahuaman lies on a mountain peak above modern Cuzco, in the High Andes of Peru. Some of the stones used in the construction of the walls are said to weigh about 200 tons each. They fit so perfectly and accurately that you cannot insert a knife blade between them.

Another example is the Gateway of the Sun at Tiahuanaco, on the Bolivian side of Lake Titicaca, 12,000 feet up in the mountains. It has on it a carved figure of the sun, surrounded by winged messengers, and also sculptured on it a precise astronomical calendar of a very unusual nature. However, apart from the Gate of the Sun itself there are other remains of a ruined city with monolithic structures consisting once again of 200-ton stones. How were these elevated to a height of 12,000 feet thousands of years ago? Or, did a sudden catastrophe which we know occurred at that time raise the whole city of Tiahuanaco up to that elevation from sea level? There is reason to suspect that this was the case because if you visit Lake Titicaca today the old shore line can still be seen. Shells and marine plants can still be found indicating that the lake was originally part of the sea.[2]

And what about the huge colossi at Easter Island? Those immense statues of giant men gazing out to sea.

There is also the huge platform at Baalbeck upon which the Romans much later built superb temples to their gods. No one has come up with the answer as to when this platform was built. Certainly the Romans were not capable of lifting such huge stones into position. On one stretch of this platform there are three immense stones, two of which are sixty-four feet long and one is sixty-nine feet long. A fourth lies a quarter of a mile away in a pit.

In the words of Mark Twain, "It lay there just as the giants of the old forgotten time left it when they were called hence, to remain for thousands of years an eloquent rebuke to such as are prone to think lightly of the men who have lived before them. This enormous block lies there squared and ready for the builders' hands, a solid mass fourteen feet by seventeen feet wide and seventy feet long."[3]

Then a sudden catastrophe shattered the world that the technological 'giants' had no control over. Our solar system was still in its raw state and unharnessed. It must have come upon us suddenly because both at Baalbeck and at Easter Island, there are signs that the work had to be hurriedly abandoned. We know, too, that in Northern Siberia the remains of mastodons have been found with undigested food in their stomachs. Their carcases were sometimes found in standing positions, indicating that death overtook them very suddenly about 15,000 years ago.

What a task it must have been for survivors of these terrible events to bring any sort of order out of such devastating chaos. Tidal waves, earthquakes and many other vicissitudes probably continued for some time before the bemused survivors could really settle down again.

A long period of primitive existence must surely have followed leading once again to the dawn of recorded history and centuries of progress up to our present day civilization. During all this time as we've seen, the flying saucers have kept watch over this planet—undoubtedly learning much themselves from witnessing our catastrophic experiences, and pondering upon the problem long and earnestly.

PART THREE

THE LANDINGS

If you shut up truth and bury it under the ground, it will but grow, and gather to itself such explosive power that the day it bursts through it will blow up everything in its way.

EMILE ZOLA

XVI

MANY SAUCER writers have suggested that the US Air Force has more than one flying saucer in its possession. And there may be some truth in this.

In June, 1947, the well-known British stage and radio star, Hughie Green, was driving across America from Hollywood to Philadelphia. He was playing his car radio to help keep himself awake, when suddenly a commentator cut in with an announcement that a flying saucer had crashed in New Mexico and that the army was moving in to investigate.[121]

The program kept being interrupted repeatedly as more and more details became known. Twiddling the dial, he managed to pick up several other local stations broadcasting the same news flash.

Upon arrival in Philadelphia, he combed through all the newspapers but not a single one carried the story. He also questioned a local radio station and drew a blank there, too. You'll grant us there's something mighty peculiar about this. The incident was hushed up. Few heard about it at all, and three years were to elapse before that particular can of beans was opened again.

In 1950, Frank Scully, a well-known newspaperman,

137

published the first book about flying saucers that ever drew considerable public attention. It was called *Behind the Flying Saucers*. It was also the first time any author had lambasted the US government to any great extent directly and indirectly on the subject of flying saucers. He literally begged the government to sue him if his material was libelous, but the government pretended not to hear a word about it. We must conclude, then, the whole thing was rigged—the government knowing all about it in advance. We must also conclude that the government had a good reason for wanting Scully's book on the market.

Here, then, was the kick off of a large international network already well past planning stage—a network that by means of undercover agents would *indirectly* control and censor to their liking all propaganda in the newspapers and elsewhere on the subject of flying saucers. Not one word of this can be proved, of course, or ever will be. Suffice it to say, after years in the field the arrows point in one direction only.

I am not suggesting that book publishers have been directly influenced in any way by the authorities or any agencies—far from it—but because no lead has been given on this important subject all sorts of sensational material has appeared which has served to cast ridicule on the flying saucers. This, of course, suits the network.

Meanwhile, the implication has been given out from certain quarters that the saucers are not nice to know. Actually, there's nothing spooky, chilling, or frightening about them—quoting Dorothy Kilgallen's adjectives on the subject, as you'll see shortly. What is spooky about metal craft that are propelled by various adaptations of electromagnetic energy?

What officialdom's object may be in this ridiculous set-up we'll explore a little later. Right now, I wish to say that although Scully's book was rumored to have been seriously ridiculed by both the press and the public, the former was certainly contrived—phoney—and the latter must have been a mere flurry because the book sold very well, indeed. Even a British edition was published in 1955.[122]

In his book, Scully had acted as spokesman for a mysterious scientist 'Dr. Gee.' (Right here is a subtle clue to network policy regarding names, because the scientist who was revealed later as none other than Silas W. Newton, could just as easily have been given the pseudonym of Dr. Whiz or Dr. Gosh by the redoubtable Frank Scully and come off giving the same general effect.)

Be that as it may, the scoop was that Dr. Gee had given a lecture to the students at the University of Denver on March 18, 1950, in which he stated that three out of four saucers which had developed propulsion troubles and made forced landings (one of them near Aztec, Mexico) had been confiscated and a number of little men found dead in them; that a group in geophysical research had inspected one of the craft and found sixteen men measuring thirty-six to forty inches in height burned to a brown crisp.

Sixteen men were also found charred beyond recognition in one of the other craft, while the third, a small ship measuring thirty-six feet in diameter and manned by a crew of only two men had died while attempting to climb out of the ship.

At the same time, it was rumored in Scully's book that originally sixteen occupants of the craft had not been found dead, but that army engineers attempting to find means of entering had finally managed to bore a small hole the size of a pencil through one of the portholes with the result that the inrushing air had killed our visitors.

This rumor appears incredibly barbaric. It is hard to imagine any army engineer so grossly stupid as to continue boring through a porthole when the passengers, if alive, would most certainly have warned them off by frantic gestures indicating what would happen when the Earth's air poured into their cabin. From the practical standpoint if not altruism, any army engineer with his head screwed on tight would have been glad to co-operate considering how much more could be learned from live passengers than dead ones.

Anyway, towards the end of Silas Newton's lecture he told the students about the discovery of a fourth saucer he and his group had stumbled upon near a government proving ground and which they had found unoccupied!

Silas Newton's personal experience may likely be the true one while the rest were trumped up for propaganda purposes. The aim to make us believe these craft are not infallible, can get into electro-mechanical difficulties, which lowers their technology a few notches and might result in making us feel our armed forces could protect us from space visitors should the need ever arise.

Another most remarkable landing report of similar significance was reported in the September 5, 1955 issue of *Stuttgarter Tageblatt.*

Oslo, Norway, September 4, 1955—Only now is a board of inquiry of the Norwegian General Staff preparing a publication of the report on the examination of the remains of a UFO crashed near Spitzbergen, presumably early in 1952. Chairman of the Board, Colonel Gernod Darnbyl, during an instruction lesson for Air Force officers stated: "The crashing of the Spitzbergen disk was highly important. Although our present knowledge does not yet enable us to solve all riddles, I am confident that these remains from Spitzbergen will prove to be of utmost importance in this respect. Some time ago a misunderstanding was caused by saying that the disk probably was of Soviet origin. *It has—this we wish to state emphatically—not been built in any country on Earth.* The materials used in its construction are completely unknown to all experts having participated in the investigation." According to the Colonel the board of inquiry is, however, not going to publish an extensive report until *some sensational facts* have been discussed with US and British experts. We should reveal what we found out, as misplaced secrecy might lead to panic.

Contrary to information from American and other sources, Second Lieutenants Brobs and Tyllensen, who have been assigned as special observers of the Arctic regions since the event at Spitzbergen, claim that flying disks have already landed in the polar regions several times. Said Lieutenant Tyllensen: "I think the Arctic is serving as a kind of air base for the unknowns especially during snow storms when we are being forced back to our bases. Shortly after such adverse weather conditions, I have seen them land and take off on three separate occasions. I noticed then that after having landed they execute a speedy rotation around their disks. A brilliant glow of light, the intensity of which being variable with regard to speed and at landing and take-off, prevents any view of the things happening behind this curtain of light and on or inside the disk itself."

Has a flying saucer crashed in Britain? Or does this following account refer possibly to the Spitzbergen one that you have just read?

This story cabled to America in May, 1955, through the International News Service's London office by Dorothy Kilgallen, a very well-known American journalist, then staff correspondent on the New York *Journal-American*, indicates that one did land and that it has been possibly examined by British scientists and airmen.

Dorothy Kilgallen's account from London is reproduced here from the *Los Angeles Examiner*. It subsequently appeared in *Flying Saucer Review*:[123]

"London, May 22—I can report today on a story which is positively spooky, not to mention chilling. British scientists and airmen, after examining the wreckage of one mysterious flying ship, are convinced these strange aerial objects are not optical illusions or Soviet inventions, but are flying saucers which originate on another planet.

"The source of my information is a British official of Cabinet rank who prefers to remain unidentified. 'We believe, on the basis of our inquiry thus far, that the saucers were staffed by small men—probably under four feet tall. It's frightening, but there is no denying the flying saucers come from another planet.'

"This official quoted scientists as saying a flying ship of this type could not have possibly been constructed on Earth. The British Government, I learned, is withholding an official report on the 'flying saucer' examination at this time, possibly because it does not wish to frighten the public.

"When my husband (Richard Kolmar, Broadway producer and radio commentator) and I arrived here for a brief vacation, I had no premonition that I would be catapulting myself into the controversy over whether flying saucers are real or imaginary. In the United States all kinds of explanations have been advanced.

"But no responsible official of the United States Air Force has yet intimated the mysterious flying ships had actually vaulted from outer space."

If we accept that Dorothy Kilgallen, a responsible journalist in good standing, was given the above information by her informant, a British official of Cabinet rank, then there must be substance to the story.

Then, if the British and Spitzbergen ones are true, possibly those referred to by Scully are also true.

A correspondent of *Flying Saucer Review* has related how he was in Cuernavaca, Mexico, in the summer of 1951. He got into conversation with some Mexican professional men. One of them, an engineer, said that he had actually helped to load a flying saucer and its dead crew into an American Flying Box-Car airplane. The saucer had come down in an uninhabited valley in the Sierra Madres.

"Ah, señor," he said, "they were handsome, those little men, with fine features and beautifully formed tiny hands. But there must have been an explosion in their craft for they were burnt black, and when I touched one's face the skin came off under my finger as though it had been cooked."[124]

A similar story in many ways to the Scully, Spitzbergen and Kilgallen ones, comes from the Italian Journal *Clypeus*,[125] which described the finding of a submerged flying saucer in the North Sea close to the coast of Germany.

A famous Norwegian scientist, Dr. Hans Larsen Loberg, was one of those called upon to investigate the discovery of the saucer. This investigation took place in Heligoland, a fortified German island.

The object was found at low tide with its dome protruding above the water. The round saucer measured thirty meters (about ninety feet) in diameter and twenty-three meters (about sixty-nine feet) in height. The external color of the disk was like aluminum but later through laboratory testing it proved to be of a substance unknown to us, although it was approximately of the same lightness. The material underwent tests in fusion. The results were astonishing. It could easily withstand temperatures at 15,000 degrees Fahrenheit, without showing any trace of melting.

The saucer was seamless, showed no signs of bolts or welding.

Dr. Loberg stated: "The cabin of the craft was closed hermetically, when we finally were able to enter, we noticed in one of the compartments there were beds similar to the portable beds in an ambulance. When we got to the next room (the sleeping quarters) an unbelievable sight met our eyes . . . for at that very moment, we saw seven 'human beings' almost one on top of the other due to the inclination of the craft to one side, at the time of impact, all the men were dead.

"Statements from other scientists as well as myself, considered their age to be approximately twenty-five to thirty years. All were severely burnt, the height of those men was approximately one meter and eighty-five cm. Their teeth were of considerable perfection."

The discovery, according to Dr Loberg, has contributed to the clearing up of certain obscure facts concerning the mystery of the UFO, and most important of all, confirms the existence of extra-terrestrial beings.

The same article in *Clypeus* stated that the Heligoland Island case is not an isolated one. Mr. Jose Rohrer, Director of Pueblo Radio and President of the Pike's Peak Broadcasting Company, related that three flying saucers were forced to a catastrophic landing by American military aircraft while flying over the State of Montana. The sole extra-terrestrial pilot who survived the crash was kept alive for about two years in an enormous incubator purposely constructed in California and transported to an isolated locality which could even be fortified.

Rohrer maintains that in order to be able to communicate with the space being, United States scientists had recourse first of all to pictures and then some linguists succeeded in teaching him to read and write in English.

Furthermore, Rohrer asserted that he had been in one of the captured flying saucers and described its characteristics. It measured thirty meters in diameter and was divided into five sections like all the space machines of that type, which (according to Rohrer) consist of giant disks, rotating around a cabin fixed in the center.

The pilots' cabins of the saucer visited by Rohrer resembled thick cylindrical tubes with hermetic lids at both ends. The atmosphere inside resulted from a composition of gases under pressure containing thirty per cent oxygen and seventy per cent helium. As motive force the saucer utilized electromagnetic turbines, creating an enormous magnetic field generated by rotating rings, and capable of propelling it at a tremendous velocity.

The variations of the fields in relation to the different speeds would explain the changes of color so often observed in saucers in flight.

Well, there is the story as published in *Clypeus*. If their informant, Mr. Rohrer, is telling the facts correctly, then the United States Air Force has quite a lot of explaining to do. They will have to give a satisfactory reason as to why they forced down three flying saucers resulting tragically in considerable loss of life. That is, if they did so at all!

The late Edward J. Ruppelt, former Head of Project Blue Book, did report, however, that the USAF had opened fire at flying saucers on a number of occasions.[7]

I do not hold any brief with these stories one way or the other. I am not suggesting that *Clypeus* published inaccuracies. I am merely passing on the facts as reported by that journal. This is something that the United States Air Force and Mr. Rohrer must confirm or deny.

However, there is undeniably a tie-in between all these things, including the Scully, Kilgallen and Heligoland stories. And the arrow consistently points towards the network rather than flying saucers. It would seem our space visitors make convenient scapegoats for worldwide politico-military business of our own.

XVII

I DO NOT think that the Flying Saucer Story would be complete without including some comments and accounts of a few of the more than 2,000 contacts that have been reported since 1947.

It is only fair to state that many of these reported contact claims are hoaxes, but nevertheless, many of them are very likely genuine, like the one related earlier in this book involving the state police officer, Lonnie Zamorra, in Socorro, New Mexico, during 1964.

A lot of people who actually believe in flying saucers seem unable to go along with the idea that one of these craft could land here and that its occupants could get out to take a look around.

Surely, this does not add up. We plan to fly to the Moon shortly and to land there. We also hope to make a manned landing on Mars and the other planets in our solar system. Why should we expect the saucers to fly for years and years around our planet without touching down?

Some critics of contactees have drawn attention to the fact that the alleged space people differ to a degree beyond credibility. One visitor is seven feet or more in height and another is only three feet tall. One is fair complexioned while another is dark. Another spaceman is long-haired and one has a crew-cut. But I feel this criticism irrelevant. After all, aside from our own endless hair styles, we have on this planet people of four different colors, many different sizes and cultures. How then, could we expect our visitors not to differ from one another?—especially if they are coming—as some people think—from more than one planet.

Another criticism frequently made is that the messages the contactees claim to have received from their visitors for humanity are of a very naïve nature. Therefore, the critics say their stories are obviously untrue.

What is so naïve about these messages? Apparently, the visitors told the contactees it was not ethical to use atomic energy for bombs, and that if this unfortunate experimenting continued it could well mean catastrophe for this planet.

Many of the visitors have been reported to be of

Christ-like nature and to have given messages to the effect that we should cease fighting and live together harmoniously. Just how naïve is that? I should say this advice was unequivocally sound.

In this connection, I would like to say a few words to those of you who are new to saucer research about the late Wilbert B. Smith.

Wilbert B. Smith passed away on December 27, 1962. He was formerly in charge of the world's first official flying saucer sighting station started by the Canadian government at Shirley Bay, near Ottawa. This was called Project Magnet. He was subsequently Superintendent, Radio Regulations Engineering, Department of Transport, Ottawa.

At one time he carried his investigations into contact stories. How he set about this I don't know. However, I can quote the results from a speech he delivered in Ottawa on March 31, 1958:[126]

"The inevitable conclusion was that it was all real enough, but that the alien science was definitely alien —and possibly even for ever beyond our comprehension. So another approach was tried—the philosophical—and here the answer was found in all its grandeur.

"I will not go into details on the many revisions in ideas and basic thinking beyond stating that the people from outside displayed great patience and understanding in overcoming the prejudices and misinformation I had spent many years in accumulating. I began for the first time in my life to realize the basic one-ness of the Universe—science, philosophy, and all that is in it. Substance and energy are all facets of the same jewel, and before any one facet can be appreciated, the form of the jewel itself must be perceived.

"One of the most important things I had to realize was that we are not alone. The human race in the form of MAN extends throughout the Universe, and is incredibly ancient. Also, its appearance in physical form is but one of the many manifestations along the path of progress.

"Our civilization here on Earth now is only one of many that have come and gone. This planet has been colonized many times by people from elsewhere, and our present human race are blood-brothers of these people. Is it any wonder that they are interested in us? To orthodox thinkers this may seem strange, but not nearly so strange as our orthodox ideas on evolution. The question might be asked—if these people are our brothers, and are interested in our welfare, why do they remain aloof? The answer is available.

"There is a basic law of the Universe which grants each and every individual independence and freedom of choice, so that he may experience and learn from his experiences. No one has the right to interfere in the affairs of others—in fact, our Ten Commandments are directives against interference. If we disregard this law, we must suffer the consequences, and a little thought will show that our present world state is directly attributable to violation of this principle. . . .

"I would like to say a few words on the philosophy of the saucers. Possibly one of the most interesting aspects of the study of flying saucers, beyond the realization that they are real and extra-terrestrial is their philosophy. What manner of creatures build and fly them? What do they look like? How do they think? Are their ideas and ideals similar to ours? Could we understand them . . . ?

"There have been many published instances of contacts between these people from outside and the people of Earth, and a great many more which have not been published. As is always the case in any new and romantic field, there are those who prevaricate and exaggerate, but it is not too difficult to establish that the vast majority are honest and authentic. For instance, when a dozen or so independent contacts, having no common connection and each alone believing that he or she has been favored above all others to receive this message, and tell the same message even to names and descriptions which tally perfectly, one has little choice but to believe that they are telling the truth. Furthermore, when the material given to us through the many channels is all assembled and analyzed, it adds up to a complete and elegant philosophy which makes our efforts sound like the beating of jungle drums.

"These people tell us of a magnificent cosmic plan, of which we are a part, which transcends the lifetime of a single person or nation or civilization, or even a planet or a solar system. We are not merely told that there is something beyond our immediate experience— we are told what it is and our relation therewith.

"Many of our most vexing problems are solved with a few words—at least, we are told of the solutions if we have the understanding, and fortitude to apply them. We are told of the inadequacies of our science, and we have been given the basic grounding for a new science, which is at once simpler and yet more embracing than the mathematical monstrosity which we have conjured up. We have been told of a way of life which is Utopian beyond our dreams, and the means of attaining it.

"Can it be that such a self-consistent and magnificent philosophy is the figment of imagination of a number of misguided morons? I do not think so. If the only evidence we had was philosophical, we might suspect it. But when coupled with the observations—thousands of them—we cannot dismiss it so easily. This is especially true when we consider that the science which has been passed to us by these people from elsewhere explains in a manner in which we have been quite unable to do, why the saucers behave as they do, and how it is that they can do things which to us are virtually impossible. The science and the performance check perfectly. Again, we have been told where our scientific ideas are wrong or inadequate, and experiments have been carried out, and in every case the alien science has been vindicated. . . ."

XVIII

MANY PEOPLE may not realize that more than five years before George Adamski—the most publicized contactee —claimed his first contact with an extra-terrestrial, another man, Jose C. Higgins, met several spacemen in a remote place in Brazil.[127]

It was on July 23, 1947, a few days after the Arnold sighting—the news of which had not yet reached Brazil, that Higgins, a topographer, who was working with a group of people in an isolated spot suddenly heard a whistling sound above him. Looking up he was struck utterly dumb with amazement to see "a strange, circular air ship" (note his words) descending out of the sky towards them.

The others who'd been with him bolted and ran, but Higgins, made of sterner stuff, remained to see what would happen next. The huge ship settled to the ground about 150 feet from him and Higgins walked over to take a good look at it. At this point, he noticed that two people were also taking a good look at him through one of the portholes. A few seconds later three other people got out of the craft.

They were dressed in the same kind of transparent suit we've heard about so often—the kind that completely covered their bodies from head to foot, and on their back was a metal box like the one described by the contactee Salvador Villanueva in Mexico during 1953.[128]

They were about seven feet tall, and apparently not at all hirsute, as they had no beards or eyebrows and little hair on their heads, yet Higgins described them as being beautiful in appearance. He was not sure whether they were men or women, saying this was something he'd never know.

Higgins tried to find out from which planet they originated. One of the visitors made a drawing on the ground of a sun with seven circles around it and kept pointing to the seventh circle, which Higgins decided meant our planet Uranus.

This is a moot question because one sun becomes as commonplace as the next to people accustomed to traveling about the galaxy (or if you prefer . . . commonplace as the next to galactic travelers), whereas we are only capable of thinking in terms of one sun—our own. There is a possibility, even if the visitor pointed to our sun in order to make the central circle in his drawing clear, he was actually referring to the sun in his native solar system instead, indicating that their planet was in seventh position from it. Amusingly enough, this would be just about right for the very hot blue-white Wolf 359. And wouldn't it be funny if the US Air Force was right?

Then Higgins had the feeling they wanted to take him along with them to see their planet and despite their friendliness he became alarmed, and immediately showed them a snapshot of his wife gesturing earnestly that he wanted to fetch her to go along on the trip, too.

They made no attempt to stop him from walking away. He retreated to a forest where he watched from a hiding place.

Now, they began stretching their bones, as we say, or taking a bit of exercise by jumping about, throwing enormous stones and generally performing extraordinary antics, much to the surprise of Higgins. (I'm sure some day our astronauts will indulge in similar activities as soon as we produce spaceships sufficiently comfortable to enable them to do an Irish jig the moment they emerge from them. Today, we heave a sigh of relief if they can walk at all after getting out of those infernally small capsules.)

It is also quite possible the space visitors were combining an experiment with pleasure to feel the difference between a planet with a greater gravitational pull than their own.

Another well-known American contactee is Daniel W. Fry, who in his book *The White Sands Incident*,[129] described how on July 4, 1950, he was taken for a ride in a remote controlled flying saucer from White Sands to New York and back in approximately thirty minutes.

Dan Fry never saw his visitor who conversed with him telepathically from the flying saucer's base ship hovering 900 miles above the Earth's surface.

At the time of this incident, Mr. Fry was a technician at White Sands Proving Ground, New Mexico.

Then, in 1952, an encounter took place four miles inside the Russian zone of Germany between an ex-mayor, Herr Linke, who was accompanied by his daughter Gabrielle, and the occupants of a flying saucer. Although this is an old story, I think it useful to include it because not only is it of interest and rings true, but is one from behind the Iron Curtain.[86]

Herr Linke was returning to the Western Zone by motor cycle with his daughter up behind him on the pillion seat. Suddenly, their back tire burst. They both jumped down and started to push the bike along the road through the woods.

It was Gabrielle who saw something strange about 150 yards ahead of them. They soon saw in the twilight as they came nearer that there were two strange figures wearing what appeared to be one-piece silvery suits. (Again one-piece suits—Author.) One of them had a light on his chest which flashed on and off.

Then Herr Linke got a tremendous shock. Behind these two eerie figures was a huge circular object lying there in the forest glade. He estimated it to be about fifty feet in diameter.

His daughter called out to him. The sound of her voice caused the two silvery figures to abandon whatever they had been looking at and run back to their craft. As soon as they were inside, the outer rim of the saucer began to glow. This behavior on the part of certain of our visitors seems very common. For instance, the Australian landing to be described later in this chapter, and another that you will recall that occurred in the South of France involving the cultivator of a lavender field related earlier.

The light now emanating from the ship enabled Linke to observe a double row of portholes. Then the glow changed color from a bluish-green to red.

There was a humming sound and the saucer rose slowly into the air. Then, gathering speed the craft disappeared with a faint whistling sound.

On February 18, 1954, Cedric Allingham had a contact with a spacecraft pilot who said he was a Martian and landed his flying saucer near Lossiemouth, Scotland.

I should emphasize that Allingham always carried a camera and binoculars with him on his walks in the countryside as his hobby was bird-watching.

At about 12:35 P.M. he first noticed the saucer and managed to take some photographs of it. These are included in his book *Flying Saucer from Mars*.[130] He then followed the craft with his binoculars until it finally disappeared.

When he had eaten his lunch Allingham continued his walk along the coast away from Lossiemouth. Then, at about five minutes past three he saw it again. This time the craft was much higher up and traveling at considerable speed. Once again, it disappeared behind some clouds.

Allingham stated that at half past three he started back slowly on the return journey to Lossiemouth. He was now highly excited and hoped he'd have another chance to see it again.

He did! It was a quarter to four when he heard a swishing sound, and lo and behold! There it was coming in towards him from across the sea. He had the presence of mind to take some more snaps with his camera before the craft landed gently some fifty yards from him.

This one was about fifty feet in diameter with two visible rows of portholes. There were three spherical objects under the ship similar to those Adamski described.

Allingham walked towards the saucer as it landed. The craft had a sliding panel door from which the pilot stepped out. He was about six feet tall and had he been dressed in our attire should have passed for an Englishman—if the Englishman, that is, had a very high forehead.

The pilot of the saucer again wore the usual one-piece suit that covered his feet. One other important observation Allingham made about the space man's appearance was that he wore some attachment in his nose, obviously connected with the problem of breathing in our atmosphere. As we've noted before this is also a very common characteristic.

Perhaps, some come from planets containing a high content of oxygen and others do not. Furthermore, some of the pilots may have become acclimatized, perhaps by landing in the more rarefied atmosphere of the Himalayas or in the polar regions.

Allingham and his visitor did not converse by telepathy like Adamski said he did on his initial contact at Desert Center, California, but instead he used his drawing pad on which he drew signs and pictures.

He drew circles to represent the orbits of the various planets in relation to the sun. In this way he was able to find out the planet from which his visitor came.

Allingham related in his book that he had a discussion with the Martian about the atom bomb, the Martian canals and the shortage of water on Mars.

When the Martian walked back to his craft Allingham took a back-view snapshot of him which is reproduced in his book, and looks very much like one of the many pictures taken of Charles Lindbergh as he walked across the field to climb into the 'Spirit of St. Louis' on that memorable morning when he took off alone for France.

There was only one witness to this contact. A surprise one even to Allingham. This was a fisherman whom he had met on the road earlier. On his way back afterwards to Lossiemouth Allingham encountered him again and learnt that the fisherman had seen the saucer and the end portion of his encounter with the pilot. The man's name was James Duncan and he wrote a statement, adding his signature, on a leaf from Allingham's pad that he had witnessed the event. A facsimile of the statement was also included in Allingham's book.

Unfortunately, no one could later locate this witness. However, he may have moved from the district. Perhaps, if he should happen to read these lines, he may come forward and substantiate Allingham's claim.

Cedric Allingham's book is most entertaining, but I think it should be stated that he was a successful writer of thrillers who wrote under a pseudonym.

Papua, New Guinea, holds one of the most authenticated and near-contact incidents in researchers' files. It was not an actual landing but contact was made by the Rev. B. Gill and the members of his mission.[131] [132]

There had been numerous sightings of flying saucers over Papua. Up till March, 1960, according to the Rev. Norman E. G. Cruttwell, of the Angelican Mission, Menapi, Papua, there had been some seventy-nine reported! The Rev. Cruttwell published a paper in March, 1960, which was circulated among UFO researchers.[133] [134] This report is of the utmost importance and probably ranks as one of the most valuable contributions to the study of flying saucers. All the witnesses of the seventy-nine sightings included in the report are people of the

155

highest integrity. For example, the first sighting report is made by Mr. T. P. Drury, who was at the time of his sighting Director of Civil Aviation in the territory of Papua, New Guinea, stationed at Port Moresby.

However, it is the visitation at Boianai that we're interested in now. Although the main events and actual contact occurred on June 27, 1959, the story really began the previous night. On that evening there were thirty-eight witnesses, of whom twenty-five signed a report made by the Rev. William B. Gill. Apart from Father Gill himself, they included five Papuan teachers and three medical assistants.

A shining object appeared about 6:45 P.M. above the mission. It came down to a height estimated at only 300 to 400 feet.

Everyone agreed that the object was circular and had legs under it. A blue light shone from the craft upwards into the sky at an angle of about forty-five degrees and everyone also agreed that four figures appeared on a kind of upper deck.

The *Australian Post* reporting this sighting stated that the ship had portholes.

There were four men altogether who appeared on top of the craft, but sometimes only one, two, or three were visible. They were surrounded by some kind of illumination from the reflected blue light shining upwards from the craft.

Father Gill reported: "They seemed to be illuminated in two ways. (a) by reflected light, as men seen working high up on a building at night caught by the glare of an oxy-acetylene torch, and (b) by this curious halo which outlined them, following every contour of their figures and yet did not touch them. In fact they seemed to be illuminated themselves in the same way as the machine was."

This is a most interesting comment and brings to mind the landing described earlier in this book by space people in 1965 in the Argentine when the Toba Indians were contacted by beings with halos.

There were several other objects accompanying the main craft. The movements of the smaller ones were most erratic, moving sometimes quickly and at other times slowly.

The next evening the visitors returned again to Boianai even earlier. On Saturday, June 27, a large spacecraft was sighted by Annie Laurie Borewa, a Papuan medical assistant, at about 6 P.M. She called Father Gill who saw the object clearly himself.

He called several other mission personnel and they all watched. Then four figures again appeared on top of the ship. Two smaller craft appeared. One over the hills and one overhead.

On the mother ship, according to Father Gill's report "two of the figures seemed to be doing something near the center of the deck. They were occasionally bending over and raising their arms as though adjusting or setting up something (not visible). One figure seemed to be standing, looking down at us."

At that time the onlookers numbered about a dozen.

Father Gill then stretched his arm above his head and waved. To their surprise the figures on the space ship did the same!

Ananias Rarata, a teacher, then waved both arms over his head and the two outside figures did the same.

Father Gill relates that both Ananias and himself continued to wave and to the great surprise and joy of the mission boys the spacemen also continued to wave back.

When it became really dark Father Gill sent for a torch and directed a series of long dashes towards the space ship. After a while the saucer acknowledged by making several wavering motions back and forth.

The Rev. Cruttwell in his paper states that "the facts of this sighting and the waving by the men and the responses to the torch signals are fully corroborated by

157

Ananias Rarata, Eric Kodowa, Mrs. (Nessie) Moi, Ilma Violet and Dulcie Freda (teachers), and many of the other witnesses in personal interview with myself."

Father Gill and his thirty-eight witnesses at Boianai were not apparently the only people to see strange things that night. The Rev. Cruttwell states that there were sightings at Giva, Baniara and Sideia, and as he puts it "amply confirm that mysterious intelligently controlled flying machines were visiting Papua on June 26-28, 1959."

Although no actual landings or conversation, as far as is known, took place between the occupants of flying saucers and Father Gill's mission we must consider this is the most authenticated story of a near-contact.

Now I would like to tell you about a remarkable landing that took place in Australia. This account has been given to me by Colin J. McCarthy, an Australian. Here is the story in his own words.

"In the early spring of 1963, in the quiet, respectable suburb of Plympton situated some three miles from the center of the city of Adelaide, South Australia, two small boys (aged nine and ten respectively) were wondering how to spend their Sunday afternoon.

"The time was 2:30 P.M. Suddenly they heard a faint swishing noise in the sky above their heads, and looking up, they were amazed to see a glowing disk-like object slowly descending towards a nearby paddock. With a quick glance at each other that said 'adventure,' they quietly sneaked towards the landing area, and hid behind an old abandoned car. They were no more than 200 feet from the mysterious object.

"As they watched, not daring to even breathe, a door on the side of the great disk opened noiselessly, and stooping slowly to avoid bumping his head, one of the occupants of the craft stepped out on to the green grass. He was tall (later estimates put him around seven feet), and was wearing a tight fitting blue-black tunic, with a purple cape attached. On his head he wore a leather-like cap fastened under his chin, and his hands were covered by large, silver studded gauntlets, from which sprouted a long tube that went around the back of his head, and finally up one nostril of his nose. His skin was colored copper red—like a person with fresh sunburn, and around his waist he wore a large belt, fitted in the front with a small control panel on which his fingers were playing continuously.

"The two lads by this time were so enthralled that they forgot to remain hidden, and the visitor saw them. With a quick movement he turned and faced the craft, looking at one of the large windows or portholes, surrounding the upper part of the bell-shaped disk. He must have made some signal, because another identically dressed figure appeared for a brief second at the window, and then was gone.

"The craft began to make a small humming sound, and the outer rim began to glow. By this time the first visitor had walked quickly back, and stepped through the opened doorway. With a slight fluttering motion— like a leaf falling from a tree—the ship lifted slightly, and then, tilting to an angle of around ten degrees, arrowed into the sky at an incredible speed.

"The two boys ran home and blurted out their story to their parents who called the police. The constabulary could find no fault in the lads' tale and were convinced they were telling the truth. To verify the incident, twenty other separate witnesses saw the object as it sped away from the paddock.

"Did two small boys, on a sleepy Sunday afternoon in Plympton, South Australia, witness the landing of a space ship from another world?"

[They probably did, but I think from the attire they described the boys had seen one too many 'Superman' films—*Author*.]

Well, there you are. There have been over 2,000 reported contact stories since 1947. I have given you only six. They have not been chosen with the idea that they are the best (with the exception of the one in Papua which is outstanding) but typical of those that have occurred all over the world.

However, they are happening all the time in every country and you may be sure that there are many that are not publicized.

XIX

Do SPACE PEOPLE walk amongst us? This is a fascinating question. It's also one that'll make people turn around and look at you in an odd way. Regardless, let us consider the question for a moment anyway.

First, you've been shown overwhelming evidence proving beyond doubt that people from neighboring solar systems have been visiting and watching us for thousands of years. Obviously, then, their technology is and has been as overwhelming as the evidence.

It would constitute no great feat for them to tune in on our radio broadcasts and television channels. As to language, over a very long period the inhabitants of these advanced civilizations have learned the many tongues of this planet, although this isn't particularly necessary, as a more advanced equivalent of the United Nations translating system is undoubtedly carried by most of their craft.

It may well be that there is some infiltration of our planet without our being aware of it. This may seem fantastic, but try to envision how very far advanced are these civilizations. Seen from this premise, it is all but fruitless to equate it from our present-day standpoints. If we have a desire to understand this, then there is nothing for us but to develop both vision and level-headed imagination, steering clear of tangential ideas that have no basis in common sense.

Flying Saucer Review,[135] carried an interesting article called 'Visitors from Afar' by Frank Burr, that dealt with the theme of space people being amongst us.

This is what he said: "There is no proof that we have living on this world some persons from outer space, but there is no proof that they do not live amongst us. They could very easily introduce themselves amongst the people of Tibet. From there they could infiltrate into many other countries and mix amongst us. It is obvious that they would be more readily acceptable to people who believe in the occult, who are not subject to being ridiculed for claiming to have seen something unusual. Their sudden appearance would not be the subject of investigation by immigration authorities or police and they could establish a right to living on Earth without having to explain where they come from. 'From far away' would be a perfectly satisfactory answer to any question as to place of origin."

Whether Tibet is still such a good place for an extra-terrestrial to start operations since the Chinese invasion is an open question. However, it is possible as Mr. Burr points out that there are many hill tribes in Tibet who have men among them who were not born in the tribes and always have come from 'far away.' They could mingle with refugees coming into India.

There are many other remote and mountainous areas in the world where flying saucers can land at night unobserved and take off again, leaving behind another alien to make his way alone in a strange world. An ideal spot would be the mountains of Donegal in Ireland, for example. However, it is truly doubtful that infiltration could be easily accomplished in highly systemized countries such as England, Russia, and the United States.

Even so, it is probable that some infiltration has been occurring for quite a long while, and like the resistance movements in France during World War II, the visitors may have friends who can arrange passports, currency and the equivalent of an escape route. There would scarcely be a language problem because anyone undertaking such a mission would undoubtedly learn the language of the country where he was going to be dropped as well as rudiments of other languages of countries he hoped to visit.

In these days of jet aircraft and easy travel, more and more foreign nationals are being seen in the capital cities of the world, London, Paris, Rome, New York and Rio de Janeiro—to name a few. These are full to running over with so many diverse nationalities and tongues that people from another planet would hardly be conspicuous.

If you unknowingly met one of them in London at a social gathering and asked in what part of the world he resided, the answer might be that he'd just recently flown in from New York or Paris. He would be telling the truth, too. What is more he'd have a passport to prove it. However, whereas this would work perfectly in so far as social functions are concerned—for a limited time—authorities in many countries have ingenious methods for cross checking passports through other government agencies. The ruse in a highly systemized country surely could not be maintained for longer than a year at most, I think.

Even so, do space people walk amongst us from time to time?

I can't prove it to you. However, I should like to give you a thought-provoking quotation from a book entitled *Men of other Planets*, by Kenneth Heur. The author was a former lecturer in astronomy at the American Museum —Hayden Planetarium.[136]

"If there have been guests from other worlds, we may be their descendants. It is possible that eons ago our ancestors came from outer space as whole beings in space ships. There may even be planetarians in our society today—men of other planets may have been clever enough to take up the language and adopt the customs of the country in which they landed. They could be here in great numbers, but we would be unconscious of their presence. Or they may be here in such extraordinary forms as to be unrecognizable." And so goes the opinion of one man.

PART FOUR

BREAK-THROUGH

You can fool some of the people all the time and, all of the people some of the time, but you cannot fool all of the people all of the time.

ABRAHAM LINCOLN
May 29, 1856

XX

YOU NOW have a glimpse of the huge dossier of evidence indicating the reality of these alien ships from other worlds.

The question most frequently asked is why aren't we, the public, told officially that the flying saucers are real. Why is the truth being withheld? This book, we think, has rather well answered that. In addition, since the people have eyes, ears and minds of their own, why is it necessary to have the sanction of officialdom who only represent a mere fractional per cent of the people?

Obviously, if the saucers were hostile and out to conquer us they would have done so long ago. From what we've seen of their technology it is also obvious that it would require only a matter of seconds for them to take over the entire globe. They have shown for decades, if not millennia, that this is not their intention. We can be sure that the American and British authorities are fully aware of this situation, as are all other governments and agencies the world over. If this were not so, they couldn't go on year after year playing 'network' games. For example, *The UFO Evidence*, Section IX,[3] states that there are two schools of thought on US Air Force secrecy about

UFOs. The first school considers that the air force has proof of UFO reality, but is keeping quiet until the public can be suitably prepared for such an announcement.

The second school tends to think secrecy is not due to any special knowledge but to differences of opinion and red tape in air force circles.

Frankly I, am of the opinion, as stated earlier, that the authorities have known of the reality of flying saucers since 1947. It is possible that they knew even before then. Furthermore, they have had almost twenty years to start an educational program to prepare the masses.

However, I do not think the US Air Force is the organization responsible for withholding information about the UFOs. I consider that the policy on UFOs comes from a much higher level and that various government agencies, including the Central Intelligence Agency (CIA) are instruments used to keep the truth withheld.

In an article published in *Saucer News*,[137] entitled *UFOs and Government Secrecy*, Mr. C. W. Fitch related how he had a conversation with the late Wilbert B. Smith, former chief of the Canadian government's Project Magnet, two years before his death.

Mr. Smith told him that it was not the US Air Force but 'a small group very high up in the government.' In the same article, Mr. Fitch described how he discovered from a book published in America during 1964, *The Invisible Government,* the name of this particular group which could well be the one referred to by Wilbert B. Smith.

I have also read this remarkable book (recently published in an English edition)[138] which shows how the CIA and other intelligence agencies take their cue from this small special group of people. It was instigated during the Truman administration and has continued to operate through those of Eisenhower, Kennedy and Johnson. It is called the 54/12 group.

There are of, course, very many reasons why the governments of the world might withhold recognition of the saucers. Let us look at some of them.

(1) *Panic*—resulting in immediate disruption of our systems. We all know what happened when a radio play about an invasion from Mars was broadcast in the USA during the late thirties. It was so realistic thousands of people panicked, and it wasn't till the following day or so that life began to settle back to normal.

In a sense, to forestall panic is valid reason enough. However, nearly twenty long years have rolled by while officialdom has made not the slightest attempt to inaugurate a *bona fide* educational program about our visitors from space.

Is it simply that they know far less about them than the people (as we suggested before) and hope to keep us just sufficiently scared to stay away from the subject while they have a chance to catch up?

Meanwhile, we have been fed a continuous diet of uncensored horror films in which space visitors are for ever depicted as everything from oozing globs of protoplasm to monsters and fiends, and in which we finally outwit all this mess by our great brain power, and either win the wars with them or forestall them altogether. Superman division!

We needn't tell you that the use of the motion picture industry to condition people to whatever aims the 'powers' have in mind is the oldest modern trick of all. In this case, it is particularly ridiculous because if the saucers did intend to make war upon us (which they don't) there is no power or technology on this Earth that could do a blessed thing about it. The people might well make it a point to shake themselves loose from TV and motion picture conditioning because they couldn't win.

Secondly, these monstrous films represent the worst possible diplomacy towards our visitors—perpetually adding insult to injury. Why insult the intelligence of a technology easily one hundred thousand years ahead of our own, which we will some day match, but never catch up to?

Or put it another way. How would we feel if we discovered after landing on their planets (and we will) that they'd spent decades conditioning their people against us? How would we feel, for example, if they'd spent millions of dollars on their equivalent of TV tapes and films depicting Colonel John Glenn as a monster? That would really set off a fireworks party! Understatement of the age.

· (2) *Political*—Possibly both East and West may be trying to capture and dissect a flying saucer to find out how it ticks. Obviously, if one side of the Iron Curtain or the other could gain the secret of saucer propulsion first, it would constitute a great deal more than just having a proverbial feather in one's cap. It would make that nation's cap look like a full Indian Chief!

However, I think it more than likely that both the Americans and the Russians already have a few experimental saucers they've painstakingly copied from watching and studying reports of sightings.

I'll stick my neck out farther and suggest that both the American and Russian governments have an understanding behind the scenes on UFO policy. These two nations may disagree on everything from point A up to point Z, but on point Z, the matter of UFOs, they probably feel it's the better part of wisdom to hold hands!

(3) *Economic*—This is a very important reason and one that may even have the backing of the visitors themselves. If the saucers are able to use some form of natural 'free energy' for their propulsion and this knowledge became available to humanity there might be economic chaos. Think of the effect on the coal, oil and electrical industries (to mention but three). If it was realized that we no longer had to rely on them to drive

our vehicles, light and heat our homes and places of work, then these industries could become obsolete overnight.

If the governments knew that saucers used free energy this could be a very strong reason for keeping the subject under wraps in order to maintain what is called economic stability.

Without doubt you can think of many more reasons why government agencies have acted and reacted so unwisely in many respects, and in general so peculiarly through the years.

The view has also been put forward that saucers have not been recognized because there was no government department in any country to deal with such a situation. This is a very interesting point of view and very plausible. It is quite true we have no governmental departments to deal with extra-terrestrial affairs. We have our Ministeries of Defence, War, Home Affairs and so on.

However, if we stop to think a moment we find flaws in this argument. I agree, of course, there are no such governmental departments. Nevertheless, if the intelligence services of various countries reported alien ships were coming into our atmosphere, someone is eventually going to take notice, and that person, if there is no government department, is going to be the Prime Minister of Great Britain, the President of the United States and the Heads of other states. Reports of that nature would go eventually to the highest authority. You can be sure that some body of people would be instructed to investigate further and report back.

Obviously, right now there is no publicized department of state looking after extra-terrestrial affairs, for which we can all thank God! Nevertheless, the subject is the concern of certain high-level people and highly classified.

I would go so far as to suggest that the American Air Force Project Blue Book and the Department in the

British Air Ministry dealing with UFO reports and inquiries from the public are both fronts. Captain Ruppelt, former Head of Project Blue Book, himself stated in his book that he was worried by this very question and also made it clear that his job was to explain as many reports by conventional means as possible. As for the others—the unknowns—it was not his job to say what they were.

It is an interesting thought that perhaps even the space people themselves do not wish to impinge their civilization on us too hurriedly.

A well-known Italian contactee, Bruno Ghibaudi, has summed up this well. Incidentally, Ghibaudi is a journalist in Turin and well-known to the Italian TV and radio public.

In an article in *Flying Saucer Review*[139] Gordon W. Creighton quotes Ghibaudi on why open contact has not yet been made, as follows:

"The *real* problem is, nevertheless, not panic at all. Our masses are not yet ready for a revelation of this kind. . . . The real problem is something quite different. Do not let us forget that between their science and ours there is a gap of thousands of years, and that for this reason an 'official' mass descent of space beings from other planets would inevitably bring about comparisons between their worlds and ours. How could such an encounter be permitted? At an inner level, we should quite certainly be severely shaken as a result of it, and they do not want to alarm us in any way. And this is all the more so, inasmuch as there are cosmic laws which prevent the more evolved races from interfering, beyond certain limits, in the evolution and development of the more backward races. For every race must be the maker of its own progress, paying the price for it with its sacrifices, its failures and its victories."

What Ghibaudi says is no doubt true, but soon we ourselves will be landing on other planets. It is high time that an educational program be started, and we have just such a plan in mind for the people—not only in mind but already begun, as you shall see immediately.

XXI

The Flying Saucer Story for our age has just begun. We have now begun the process of being groomed to take up adult responsibilities in our crowded celestial apartment house development—the entire Milky Way Galaxy.

It is the oldest story in the universe. The process goes on everywhere. But, for our time, our age, it is new. And to complement this, new space people with far more advanced technologies and spacecraft to match, who have never before visited Earth, are coming in once in a great while to look us over and to see how we're coming along—an intergalactic field service.

We have millions of planet-neighbors in this galaxy alone, and as we've said before no two planets are just alike, no harnessing or remodeling job is identical; and whereas remodeling habitable planets in a raw galaxy is essential to preserve life, care must always be taken to preserve the native individuality of each so that the artistry of all Creation remains intact.

Intersolar field services, then, have their work cut out for them, too, co-ordinating activities and keeping an eagle eye on the whole.

Just as there are no two planets alike, there are also no two people alike, nor any two animals alike, nor even two blades of grass that are identical anywhere in the universe. And as Earth people discovered this natural law they naturally created a form of government embodying the principle of it. They called it a republic. The only clue to its meaning that I can see lies in its last six letters, p-u-b-l-i-c.

This form of government is based on the sound principle that since there are no people alike anywhere, by your own individuality (which is eternal) you are called upon to represent yourself. No other man can truly represent you, or usurp your place. But, if one is to represent oneself then that individual must be able to communicate instantaneously with all other people in the whole world, and eventually with all other people in the whole galaxy, and after that with all the people in neighboring galaxies and so on throughout the universe.

Obviously, this is impossible to do without very highly advanced electronic communication systems. One cannot speak *personally* with each individual everywhere, but through two-way electronics communication one can speak *impersonally* to everyone in the world and hear his replies within the hour by means of worldwide electronic tabulation, and in this manner the people of the world become as ONE MAN 'indivisible and indestructible.'

The groundwork for republics has been laid in many countries throughout the world. The United States of America was founded on it, but it, too, had to await the *necessary machinery* to carry it out, which it never had until today. In the meantime, while waiting for the technology to catch up to this sound natural law (principle), democracies had to be inaugurated in the place of republics in which the people elect representatives to speak for them! It's a make-do until you can have the *real thing!*

There's no mystery now why a democracy cannot survive for any length of time. It's merely a lean-to while you're waiting for the main structure to be built. No mystery now why a dictatorship form of government cannot survive either, and its days are even fewer in number. With these, it's like trying to survive in a pup-tent while you're waiting for the real thing to begin.

The problem of instant communication has never been one to plague our space visitors, at least not for eons. With this problem solved one automatically falls into a republic form of government, because it merely follows basic natural law. In this way, federations of republics from one solar system to the next blossom overnight without campaigns, stupid political harangues, ideologies by the dozens, and all the phoney claptrap on the subject we've been forced to endure on this planet.

On this point alone lies another reason our space neighbors refuse to communicate with Earth governments *en masse*, preferring to seek out private individuals here and there with the hope that by our watching them (without their undue interference in Earthly affairs) *the people* will suddenly grasp the meaning and eternality of their own personal heritage, and through proper use of electronics become the impersonal voice of *one man* on a world-wide *one world basis*.

At this point in our progress, we will automatically and spontaneously be ready to speak with all our space neighbors in this celestial apartment house development we call the Milky Way. For the first time in Earth's history the horse will be ahead of the cart and not behind it.

Electronically we are in a position to begin now. We are in a position to validify a natural, sound, abstract law. An abstract, however perfect and wonderful, is nothing until it has been validified and carried out in three dimensional form, and that's another reason why we're here. And because of that very reason, too, our space neighbors hover and fly about us almost constantly as a very quiet reminder that fairly shouts:

"Come on Earth!
You can make it!
Join the galaxy!"

To hasten this day a world-wide organization has been formed called INTERNATIONAL SKY SCOUTS. It welcomes all young people the world over who wish to participate and learn the rudiments of 'field service.'

Because each boy and girl is an individual possessing individual gifts and talents, each is encouraged to follow them. Some young people may be far more fascinated with the job of taming the raw currents in the Earth beneath their feet. Others may be drawn to the study of the ocean, or space, while others may find the mysteries of our sun more fascinating than anything else, and wish to include in that the general subject of astronomy.

Whatever the talent, you may be sure it fits into the over-all galactic picture and is not only needed but indispensable.

To this will be added round table discussions—an exchange of information—and a clearing house for this exchange. There will be impromptu lectures on subjects of greatest interest, whether the interest of the moment happens to center about deoxyribonucleic acid (DNA) or our space neighbors and their craft. Our space neighbors will act as guides, hosts to the feast of subjects, by films that will be shown of them in flight, and an exchange of everything that we know about them and learn by watching them. We then apply what we learn —correlate it—to our own particular field of interest.

Since our space neighbors follow basic natural laws harnessed and tamed constructively to do their bidding, these basic principles yield themselves readily to any constructive endeavor under our sun, and can be utilized by any subject at all, although on the surface these subjects may seem to be as unrelated as music, biology and space mechanics. Don't be fooled. They aren't.

One of the rudiments of 'field service' is the art of correlating all seemingly dissimilar subjects in both arts and sciences. Some young people may have a special gift for just this one work alone.

All this may sound as though we're not concentrating very heavily on our space neighbors and their ships. That's right. We aren't! You see, they are not an escape, or an escape route from ourselves or the reality of our business in this world. They are not here to supply a thrill for a bored or weary mind. As we apply ourselves wholeheartedly to the development of our own special talents and extend those outward to care for the needs of our environment, and as we lose ourselves inside our interests and talents, we will suddenly find our space neighbors right beside us without taking any thought for it at all.

The quickest route to the stars and our neighbors throughout the galaxy lies right under our feet and within the development of ourselves. We can better spread the knowledge and reality of their existence in this way than in any other. They are quite real. They are not *trying to be* something, they *are* something. And herein lies the clue to *being* with them.

VIPs TALKING ABOUT THE SAUCERS

POLITICIANS

I can assure you that flying saucers, given that they exist, are not constructed by any power on Earth.

EX-PRESIDENT TRUMAN
(Press Conference, April 4, 1950)

I do not think it would be correct to say they come from a planet (that is, from one single planet as General Twining said).

EX-PRESIDENT EISENHOWER
(Press Conference, November 1954)

Flying saucers—unidentified flying objects—or whatever you call them are real.

FORMER US SENATOR BARRY GOLDWATER
Air Force Reserve Colonel

It is a phenomenon which interests all humanity.

ENGELO CERICO
Former President of Defence Commission
of Italian Senate

MILITARY

The existence of these machines is evident and I have accepted them absolutely.

AIR CHIEF MARSHAL LORD DOWDING

If they should come from Mars we should not be frightened.

GENERAL TWINING
(During a talk to pilots at Amarillo Base
on May 15, 1954)

176

THE FLYING SAUCER STORY

Reliable reports indicate there are objects coming into our atmosphere at very high speeds and controlled by thinking intelligences.

ADMIRAL DELMER FAHRNEY
Former American Navy Missile Chief
(Press Conference, January 16, 1957)

For if we persist in refusing to recognize the existence of these unidentified objects, we will end up, one fine day, by mistaking them for the guided missiles of an enemy, and the worst will be upon us.

GENERAL L. M. CHASSIN
Former General Air Defence Coordinator
Allied Air Forces, Central Europe (NATO)
(Extract from preface to book *Flying Saucers and the Straight Line Mystery*, by Aimé Michel)

However, there have remained a percentage of the total in the order of twenty per cent of the reports that have come from credible observers of relatively incredible things.

GENERAL JOHN SAMFORD
Former Director of Intelligence, US Air Force
(Press Conference, July 29, 1952)

One thing is absolutely certain. We're being watched by beings from outer space.

ALBERT M. CHOP
Former Air Force press official handling UFO information at the Pentagon

Many times I have seen flying disks following and overtaking missiles in flight at the experimental base at White Sands, New Mexico, where, as is known, the first American atom bomb was tried out.

COLONEL MACLAUGHLIN
Missile expert
(Statement in 1949)

THE FLYING SAUCER STORY

What constitutes proof? Does a UFO have to land at the River Entrance to the Pentagon, near the Joint Chiefs of Staff offices? Or is it proof when a ground radar station detects a UFO, sends a jet to intercept it, the jet pilot sees it, and locks on with his radar, only to have the UFO streak away at phenomenal speed? Is it proof when a jet pilot fires at a UFO and sticks to his story even under the threat of court-martial. Does this constitute proof?

CAPTAIN EDWARD J. RUPPELT
Former Head of the US Air Force Project Blue Book
(Extract from preface to his book,
The Report on Unidentified Flying Objects

It is a calculated risk to assume that the so-called saucers do not constitute a threat to the welfare and security of our citizens. We are given to believe they are not hostile, but information on UFOs is classified.

COLONEL FRANK MILANI
Director of Civil Defense, Baltimore, Md.

SCIENTISTS

It is possible that the saucers come from Venus using the side of the Moon invisible to Earth as a base.

DR. WALTER RIEDEL
Late Director of Peenemunde Base, Germany

I believe extra-terrestrial intelligences are watching the Earth and have been visiting us for millenia in their flying saucers.

DR. HERMANN OBERTH
Famous rocket scientist

Flying saucers come from another world.

PROFESSOR HIDEO ITOKAWA
Japanese scientist

178

THE FLYING SAUCER STORY

They were strange, terrifically fast. I think the government should set up a twenty-four hour alert with radar, telescope, sky cameras and other instruments.

DR. J. J. KALIZKEWSKI
*Cosmic ray scientist on navy project, who with
other scientists sighted two cigar-shaped UFOs
near Minneapolis*

I do believe there are objects that are unidentified.

DR. CARL SAGAN
(A talk to the American Rocket Society during 1962)
*Distinguished astronomer at the University of California,
member of the Space Biology Advisory Committee, NASA,
and National Academy of Sciences and the Armed Forces
Panel on extra-terrestrial life*

AIRCRAFT AND EQUIPMENT MANUFACTURERS

The disks use a means of propulsion different from ours. There is no other possible explanation. Flying saucers come from another world.

LOUIS BREGUET
French aircraft manufacturer

I believe the flying saucers come from outer space, piloted by beings of superior intelligence.

WILLIAM LEAR
*President, Lear Inc. (maker of aircraft and
electronics equipment)*

PILOTS

Flying saucers have an extra-terrestrial origin. Neither Americans nor Russians are capable of constructing machines of this sort. The characteristics of the disks are clearly superior to present possibilities of science.

PIERRE CLOSTERMANN
French air ace

It must have been some weird form of spaceship from another world.

CAPTAIN JAMES HOWARD
BOAC pilot whose sighting of a huge UFO and six smaller ones is described in this book

I believe the disks were intelligently controlled machines from outer space.

CAPTAIN W. B. NASH
Pan American Airways (with his co-pilot he saw a formation of six huge disks)

Before then, I wasn't convinced by the saucer reports. Now I know they do exist.

CAPTAIN RICHARD ADICKES
TWA pilot who with crew and seven passengers saw a glowing UFO pacing their airliner near South Bend

This was absolutely real. I'm convinced there was something fantastic up there.

CAPTAIN RAYMOND RYAN
American Airlines pilot who with forty-four passengers was asked by Griffiths Air Force Base to chase a UFO between Albany and Syracuse and to report by radio

These extra-terrestrial explorers are separated from us by a gigantic barrier higher than the Himalayas—which is our retarded technical knowledge and our haughty ignorance.

GABRIEL VOISIN
Pioneer of French aviation

THE ARTS

The astonishing thing would be if they did not exist.

JEAN COCTEAU
Famous poet, member of the Académie française.
He died on October 11, 1963

APPENDIX

INTERNATIONAL SKY SCOUTS*

The International Sky Scouts now number over 50,000 and are growing at a very rapid rate. They operate in countries all over the world.

Readers in the United States wishing to join should write to:

> Don Karr,
> 626 Broadway,
> Cincinnati 2,
> Ohio - 45202
> U.S.A.

Readers in other countries should write to the International Chairman if they wish to become Sky Scouts and should state if they wish to form National Associations in their own countries. They should write to:

> The Hon. Brinsley Le Poer Trench,
> Flat 8,
> 57 Drayton Gardens,
> London, S.W.10.,
> England

---

*Please note that International Sky Scouts have no connection with the world-wide Boy Scout movement.

BIBLIOGRAPHY

1 Moore, Patrick 'Communication with Other Worlds,' *The Listener and BBC Television Review* August 12, 1965.

2 Le Poer Trench, B. *Men Among Mankind* Neville Spearman, London, 1962.

3 Hall, Richard Editor, *The UFO Evidence* published by the National Investigations Committee on Aerial Phenomena (NICAP), Washington, 1964.

4 *Unidentified Flying Objects* A documentary film released through United Artists.

5 *Flying Saucer Review* London, Vol I No 1 (Spring 1955) p2.

6 Arnold, Kenneth, and Palmer, Ray *The Coming of the Saucers* privately published by the authors, Amherst, Wisconsin, 1952.

7 Ruppelt, Edward J. *The Report on Unidentified Flying Objects* Doubleday, New York, 1956.

8 Wilkins, Dr. H. Percy *Mysteries of Space and Time* Frederick Muller, London, 1955.

9 Wilkins, Harold T. *Flying Saucers on the Moon* Peter Owen, London.

10 FSR Vol 2 No 1 (January-February 1956), p2.

11 Michel, Aime *The Truth about Flying Saucers* Criterion Books, New York, 1956.

12 Keyhoe, Donald E. *Flying Saucers from Outer Space* Hutchinson, London, 1954.

13 Girvan, Waveney *Flying Saucers and Commonsense* Frederick Muller, London, 1955.

14 *Sunday Dispatch,* November 17, 1954.

15 Howard, Captain James 'We were shadowed from Outer Space' *Everybody's Weekly* London, December 11, 1954.

16   FSR Vol 1 No 4 (September-October 1955), p29.

17   ——Vol 4 No 3 (March-April 1956), p3.

18   *Diario Illustrado* Lisbon, November 16, 1957.

19   Ferreira, Captain Jose Lemos 'Air Force pilots spend forty minutes with saucers' FSR Vol 4 No 3 (May-June 1958), pp.2-3.

20   FSR Vol 4 No 1 (January-February 1958), p3.

21   ——Vol 5 No 1 (January-February 1959), pp 6-7.

22   *Correio da Manha* Rio de Janeiro, February 21, 1958.

23   Lorenzen, Coral 'Brazilian official report on the Trinidad UFO' *Fate* (USA) magazine, March 1963, pp. 38-48.

24   FSR Vol 5 No 5 (September-October 1959), p2.

25   Creighton, Gordon W. 'Unidentified Satellites' FSR Vol 7 No 1 (January-February 1961), pp. 3-6.

26   FSR Vol 9 No 3 (May-June 1963), p20.

27   Llewellyn, John D. 'Mystery Satellites' FSR Vol 9 No 6 (November-December 1963), p15.

28   *Daily Telegraph* September 3, 1960.

29   Keyhoe, Donald E. *The Flying Saucer Conspiracy* Henry Holt & Co., New York, 1957.

30   *Evening News* June 19, 1961.

31   FSR Vol 7 No 5 (September-October 1961), pp. 27-28.

32   *Melbourne Sun* August 15, 1961.

33   FSR Vol 8 No 5 (September-October 1962), p4.

34   ——Vol 8 No 6 (November-December 1962), pp. 6-9.

35   Cramp, Leonard G. 'A Challenge to the Technical Press' FSR Vol 9 No 1 (January-February 1963), pp. 6-10 and p iii of cover.

36   FSR Vol 9 No 2 (March-April 1963), pp. 7-8.

37   Manchester *Daily Express* June 20, 1962.

38   *Today* Magazine September 22, 1962.

39   *Yorkshire Post* August 25, 1962.

40   *Sheffield Telegraph* August 30, 1962.

41   Girvan, Waveney 'The Wiltshire Crater Mystery' FSR Vol 9 No 5 (September-October 1963), pp. 3-8.

42   Bainbridge, John   'Notes on the Dufton Fell Crater'
FSR Vol 9 No 6 (November-December 1963), p17.

43   Lord, Harry B. 'Seven Possible Landings,' *Orbit*,
Vol 5 No 2 pp. 2-9.

44   Stickland, Charles 'Crater Mystery—What happened at Charlton?' BUFOA Journal, London, N1. Summer
1963, pp. 12-15.

45   Southern, John   'Charlton Confession' BUFOA Journal, No 2 Autumn, 1963, p15.

46   *Yorkshire Post* July 27, 1963.

47   FSR Vol 10 No 4 (July-August 1964), pp. 18-19.

48   —Vol 10 No 6 (November-December 1964), pp.
6-7. Reprinted from *The UFO Investigator* (July-August
1964), published by NICAP, Washington.

49   Lorenzen, Coral 'UFO lands in New Mexico,' *Fate*
Magazine (USA), August 1964. pp. 27-38.

50   FSR Vol 10 No 5 (September-October 1964), pp.
22-23.

51   Hotchkiss, Olga M.   'New York UFO and its "Little
People" ' *Fate* Magazine (USA), September 1964. pp. 38-42.

52   *Cordoba* Argentina, February 25, 1965.

53   Creighton, Gordon W.   'A Russian Wall Painting and
other "spacemen" ' FSR Vol 11 No 4 (July-August 1965),
pp. 11-13.

54   FSR Vol 11 No 5 (September-October 1965), quoting from *The Herald* Australia, July 17, 1965, and the
Dundee Courier Scotland, July 19, 1965.

55   *The Flying Saucer News* published by CIBA International, Yokohama, Japan. Vol 8 No 8, p6.

56   *Pacific Stars and Stripes* March 21, 1965.

57   *The Japan Times* March 21 and 24, 1965.

58   *The Mainichi Daily News* March 22 and 24, 1965.

59   *Asaki Evening News* March 27, 1965.

60   *Nice Matin* July 3, 1965.

61   *L'Espoir* July 4, 1965.

62   Bowen, Charles 'A Significant Report from France',
FSR Vol 11 No 5 (September-October 1965), pp. 9-11.

63 Adamski, George *Inside the Space Ships* Abelard-Schuman, New York, 1955.

64 *Daily Telegraph* London, May 12, 1962.

65 *Daily Mail* London, May 12, 1962.

66 *Le Matin* Paris, May 13, 1962.

67 FSR Vol 8 No 4 (July-August 1962), pp. 3-4 and 13.

68 *Daily Telegraph* London, May 24, 1962.

69 *Time* Magazine, July 27, 1962.

70 FSR Vol 8 No 5 (September-October 1962), p26.

71 ——Vol 11 No 5 (September-October 1965), p3.

72 *The Times* London, June 5, 1965.

73 *The Daily Mirror* London, June 5, 1965.

74 Creighton, Gordon W. 'Foo Fighters' FSR Vol 8 No 2 (March-April 1962), pp. 11-15.

75 FSR Vol 3 No 6 (November-December 1957), p8.

76 Chichester, Francis *The Lonely Sea and The Sky* Hodder & Stoughton, London, 1964.

77 Roerich, Nicholas *Altai-Himalaya* Fred Stokes, New York, 1929.

78 Thomas, Paul *Flying Saucers through the Ages* Neville Spearman, London, 1966.

79 Alexander, M. 'UFO—seen by Sixty thousand' FSR Vol 4 No 1 (January-February 1958), pp. 10-11.

80 Ribera, Antonio 'What happened at Fatima?' FSR Vol 10 No 2 (March-April 1964), pp. 12-14.

81 Inglefield, Sir Gilbert S. 'Fatima, The Three Alternatives' FSR Vol 10 No 3 (May-June 1964), pp. 5-6.

82 Vallee, Jacques *Anatomy of a Phenomenon* Henry Ragnery Company, Chicago, 1965.

83 Fort, Charles *The Books of Charles Fort* published for the Fortean Society by Henry Holt and Company, New York, 1941.

84 *The Encyclopaedia Britannica* 11th Edition.

85 FSR Vol 10 No 6 (November-December 1964), p32 and p iii of cover.

86 Leslie, Desmond and Adamski, George *Flying Saucers have Landed* Werner Laurie, London, 1953.

87 *Chicago Record* April 2, 1897.

88 Williamson, G. H. *Other Tongues—Other Flesh* Amherst Press, Amherst, Wisconsin, 1963.

89 *L'Astronomie* 1885, p349.

90 Matthew of Paris *Historia Anglorum.*

91 De Gabalis, Compte *Discourses*, 1670.

92 Drake, W. R. 'Spacemen in the Middle Ages' FSR Vol 10 No 3 (May-June 1964), pp. 11-13.

93 —'UFOs over Ancient Rome' FSR Vol 9 No 1 (January-February 1963), p12.

94 *Doubt* the magazine of the Fortean Society in New York.

95 Sullivan, Walter *We are not Alone* Hodder & Stoughton, London, 1965.

96 Maney, Professor Charles A. 'A New Dimension in UFO Phenomena' FSR Vol 4 No 3 (May-June 1958), pp. 12-15.

97 FSR Vol 3 No 6 (November-December 1957), pp. 12-15.

98 —Vol 4 No 1 (January-February 1958), p2.

99 Maney, Professor Charles A. 'The Phenomena of Angel Hair' FSR Vol 2 No 6 (November-December 1956), pp. 16-18 and 31.

100 Wilson, George C. 'A Partial Solution to the UFO Problem' in three parts. *Flying Saucers* (Amherst Press, Wisconsin, USA), April 1964, pp. 61-68; April 1965, pp. 16-19; and August 1965, pp. 13-16.

101 Velikovsky, Dr. Immanuel *Worlds in Collision* Macmillan, America, 1950, subsequently republished by Doubleday.

102 FSR Vol 3 No 4 (July-August 1957), p15.

103 —Vol 3 No 5 (September-October 1957), p9.

104 Gilbert, William *De Magnete, magneticisque corporibus, et de magna magnete tellure* London, 1600.

105 Michel, Aime *Flying Saucers and the Straight-Line Mystery* Criterion Books, New York, 1958.

106 Watkins, Alfred *The Old Straight Track* Methuen, London, 1925.

107 Goddard, J. 'New Light on Ancient Tracks' FSR Vol 10 No 2 (March-April 1964), pp. 15-16.

108 Williamson, G. H. *Road in the Sky* Neville Spearman, London, 1959.

109 Crawford, Alan E. 'Piezoelectricity' *Discovery* magazine November 1964, pp. 28-33.

110 Cady, W. G. *Piezoelectricity* McGraw-Hill.

111 Megaw, H. D. *Piezoelectricity in Crystals* Methuen.

112 Mason, W. F. *Piezoelectricity Crystals and their Application to Ultrasonics* Van Nostrand.

113 Maney, Professor Charles A. 'Scientific Measurement of UFOs' *Fate* (USA), June 1965, pp. 31-39.

114 FSR Vol 8 No 2 (March-April 1962), p18 and p. iv of cover.

115 Thomson, Thomas *Lufora Bulletin* (March-April 1962).

116 Webb, Wells Alan *Mars the New Frontier.*

117 Oberth, Professor Hermann 'They Come from Outer Space' FSR Vol 1 No 2 (May-June 1955), pp. 12-15.

118 FSR Vol 5 No 1 (January-February 1959), p5.

119 Swift, Jonathan *Gulliver's Travels* 1726.

120 Good, I. J. 'Life Outside the Earth' *The Listener and BBC Television Review* June 3, 1965.

121 FSR Vol 1 No 1 (Spring 1955), p3.

122 Scully, Frank *Behind the Flying Saucers* Victor Gollancz, London, 1955.

123 FSR Vol 1 No 3 (July-August 1955), p6.

124 —Vol 2 No 1 (January-February 1956), p3.

125 *Clypeus*, via San Secondo 15, Torino (401), Italy, January 1965.

126 Smith, Wilbert B. A Speech. FSR Vol 9 No 5 (September-October 1963), pp. 13-16.

127 FSR Vol 7 No 6 (November-December 1961). 'The Spacemen threw Stones' reprinted from APRO Bulletin, May 1961.

128   Leslie, Desmond   'Mexican Taxi Driver meets Saucer Crew' FSR Vol 2 No 2 (March-April 1956), pp. 8-11.

129   Fry, Daniel W.   *The White Sands Incident* New Age Publishing Co., Los Angeles, 1954.

130   Allingham, Cedric   *Flying Saucer from Mars* Frederick Muller, London, 1954.

131   FSR Vol 5 No 5 (September-October 1959), pp. 6-7.

132   —Vol 5 No 6 (November-December 1959), pp. 7-8.

133   Cruttwell, Revd. Norman E. G.   *Flying Saucers over Papua. A Report* March 1960. Privately circulated.

134   —'What happened in Papua in 1959' FSR Vol 6 No 6 (November-December 1960), pp. 3-7.

135   Burr, Frank   'Visitors from Afar' FSR Vol 9 No 2 (March-April 1963).

136   Heur, Kenneth   *Men of other Planets* Gollancz, London, 1951.

137   Fitch, C. W.   'UFOs and Governmental Secrecy' *Saucer News* Vol 11 No 4 (December 1964).

138.   Wise, David and Ross, Thomas B.   *The Invisible Government* Jonathan Cape, London, 1965.

139   Creighton, Gordon W.   'The Italian Scene—Part 3' FSR Vol 9 No 3 (May-June 1963), pp. 18-20.

140   Lloyd, Dan   'Things are hotting up in the Antarctic' FSR Vol 11 No 5 (September-October 1965), pp. 4-5.

Additional Sources Consulted

Hoyle, Fred.   *Of Men and Galaxies* Heinemann Educational Books Ltd., London, 1965.

O'Neill, John J.   *Prodigal Genius. The Life of Nikola Tesla* Ives Washburn, Inc. New York, 1944.

Strong, James   *Flight to the Stars* Temple Press Books, London, 1965.

Addresses of UFO journals mentioned

APRO BULLETIN, 4145 E. Desert Place, Tucson, Arizona, USA.

BUFOA JOURNAL (now The BUFORA JOURNAL and BULLETIN), 3 Devenish Road, Weeke, Winchester, Hants, England.

CLYPEUS, via San Secondo 15, Torino (401), Italy.

FLYING SAUCER NEWS, THE, CBA International, Naka . PO Box 12, Yokohama, Japan.

FLYING SAUCER REVIEW, 21 Cecil Court, Charing Cross Road, London, WC2, England.

FLYING SAUCERS, Amherst, Wisconsin, USA.

LUFORO BULLETIN. Ceased publication. BUFORA JOURNAL listed above caters for its readership.

ORBIT, 41 Denham Gardens, Fenham, Newcastle-upon-Tyne 5, England.

SAUCER NEWS, PO Box 163, Fort Lee, N. J., USA.

UFO INVESTIGATOR, THE, 1536 Connecticut Avenue, NW, Washington, DC, USA (a NICAP publication).

THEY WALK BY NIGHT   K-300 — 50¢

by Michael Hervey

In book form for the first time, the spine-tingling, *true* accounts of creatures from "out there":

• He cursed his executioners aloud—after his head was severed from his body!

• He ministered to plane crash victims — without leaving footprints in the snow!

• He took a leave of absence — from his coffin in the graveyard!

STRANGE POWERS OF THE MIND   K-296 — 50¢

by Warren Smith

Eyewitness accounts and documented case histories of *mankind's most bizarre talents:*

• The man who reads tomorrow's headlines today!

• The woman who "saw" the Speck killings!

• The strange case of murder by hypnosis!
  Plus many other amazing enigmas!